"Why do you have a dolly, Miss Barnes?"

"This is no ordinary dolly, Master Alistair," Sarah explained. "This is a Christmas angel, given to me by my mother when I was very small."

"A Christmas angel?" asked Melissa, Alistair's five-year-old sister.

"Yes. Mama said if you squeezed your eyes closed and wished very hard, sometimes your wish would come true at Christmas. Do you have something to wish for?"

Finally, Melissa said, "I do."

"What would you wish for, Melissa dear?"

"I would wish for a new mama."

"Would that be your wish also, Alistair?" Sarah asked in a curiously gentle voice.

"I just wish for our father to love us again," he said gruffly.

Regency England: 1811-1820

*"It was the best of times,
it was the worst of times...."*

As George III languished in madness, the
pampered and profligate Prince of Wales led the
land in revelry and the elegant Beau Brummel set
the style. Across the Channel, Napoleon continued
to plot against the English until his final exile to
St. Helena. Across the Atlantic, America renewed
hostilities with an old adversary, declaring war on
Britain in 1812. At home, Society glittered, love
matches abounded and poets such as Lord Byron
flourished. It was a time of heroes and villains, a
time of unrelenting charm and gaiety, when entire
fortunes were won or lost on a turn of the dice and
reputation was all. A dazzling period that left its
mark on two continents and whose very name
became a byword for elegance and romance.

Books by Judith Stafford

HARLEQUIN REGENCY ROMANCE

Don't miss any of our special offers. Write to us at the
following address for information on our newest releases.

Harlequin Reader Service
P.O. Box 1397, Buffalo, NY 14240
Canadian address: P.O. Box 603,
Fort Erie, Ont. L2A 5X3

SARAH'S ANGEL

Judith Stafford

Harlequin Books

TORONTO • NEW YORK • LONDON
AMSTERDAM • PARIS • SYDNEY • HAMBURG
STOCKHOLM • ATHENS • TOKYO • MILAN
MADRID • WARSAW • BUDAPEST • AUCKLAND

ISBN 0-373-31211-3

SARAH'S ANGEL

Copyright © 1993 by Judy Russell Christenberry.

Printed in U.S.A.

PROLOGUE

THE TALL, broad-shouldered figure paused at the open door and stared curiously around him. Turning to leave, he was halted by the lilting voice of his eldest child, Alistair, six years of age.

"Why do you have a dolly, Miss Barnes? Are you not too old?"

The voice came from the far end of the schoolroom where a door stood partially open, leading to the governess's quarters. The man moved closer.

"Ah, this is no ordinary dolly, Master Alistair," the governess explained, her voice low and musical. "This is a Christmas angel, given to me by my mother when I was very small."

"A Christmas angel?" asked Melissa, Alistair's five-year-old sister.

"Yes, a Christmas angel. Mama said if you squeezed your eyes closed and wished very hard, sometimes your wish would come true at Christmas."

After a moment of silence, Alistair demanded, "When is Christmas?"

"A little more than a month away. Do you have something to wish for?"

The man leaned closer, as if eager to hear the children's response.

Finally, Melissa said, "I do."

"What would you wish for, Melissa, dear?"

"I would wish for a new mama."

The man's features drew together in pain and he held his breath.

"Would that be your wish also, Alistair?" the governess asked in a gentle voice.

The child's reply was gruff. "I just wish for our father to love us again."

CHAPTER ONE

SARAH BARNES leaned her cheek against the small head resting on her bosom. Justin, three years old, was not really one of her charges, as he was too young for the schoolroom, but Nanny allowed him to join his brother and sister occasionally.

"That is a wonderful drawing, Justin," she praised him. "I think your horse is most lifelike."

"*I* think it looks like a pig," Melissa said with a giggle.

Before the youngest child could erupt into protest, Sarah asked her two students a question that prompted more work. She also gave Justin a consoling cuddle.

The two little heads bent over the table, both dark like their father's, drew a smile from Sarah. The position as governess to Squire Whitfield's children was her first. She had been concerned about her abilities, and also about what treatment she would receive. The result had been felicitous in both instances.

She had found children who needed her love as much as she needed theirs. The pain of the past two years, from both her parents' deaths and a broken heart, had caused her to long for that tender emotion. In the four months she had been at Whitfield House, she and the children had formed a little family.

The only fly in the ointment was her employer. Not that he was nasty to her, or chased her around the house, as she had heard some masters were wont to do. No, the difficulty was that he ignored his children. Or he had until recently.

"Miss Barnes, shall I write my letters?" Alistair asked, his earnest face waiting for her response.

"Yes, Alistair. And Melissa, you should do so, as well."

"I'd rather draw pictures, like Justin."

Sarah smiled but remained firm. Melissa would be a heartbreaker by the time she reached the age of sixteen. Sarah hoped to teach her the important things in life before men turned her head.

"Shall I draw a dog?" Justin asked, filled with importance because he was allowed to draw when Melissa was not.

"Yes, please, my sweet, draw me a picture of Wiggins," Sarah agreed, though she knew the picture would resemble his earlier one of a horse.

She ruffled his blond hair. He seemed to be the only one of the three children to have his mother's colouring, judging by the painting in the morning-room. Mrs. Whitfield, who had died more than a year ago, had been a beauty, dearly loved by her husband, if the servants were to be believed.

"Am I interrupting?" a deep voice demanded from the doorway.

With a squeal of delight, Melissa jumped from her chair and raced across the room to throw herself in her father's arms. Alistair watched with large eyes, but he didn't move from his place.

Sarah's heart ached for the oldest child. She knew how much he longed for his father's touch, his approval. "Good morning, Mr. Whitfield. Have you come to see how well the children are progressing? Alistair is particularly good at making his letters."

She watched as he crossed the room, Melissa held in his arms, and stopped beside Alistair. He reached out to caress his son's head as he examined the child's work. The joy that passed over Alistair's face prompted Sarah to forgive her aloof employer anything.

When he had interviewed her, Sarah hadn't been sure he'd even seen her. His questions had been few and of relative unimportance. His decision to hire her had been just as casual. Even though she wanted the position, she had resented his cavalier attitude on behalf of the as yet unseen children.

During her employment, she had scarcely encountered him. She had been able to discard the padding and rice powder to make herself unattractive, a necessity for a young woman alone in the world. She would not have been hired had she not worn such a disguise. Still, she detested the neglect he showed his children.

"May I join you for a few moments, Miss Barnes? I should like to speak to my children."

His deep voice drew her back to the present. "Of course, sir. I shall wait in my room, if you desire to speak with them alone."

"No, no, you must hear my words also, as they will affect you, as well."

She looked into his grey eyes, wariness filling her. Was she to be dismissed after so short a time? Her heart tightened in fear of having to leave the children she'd come to love. Even Justin realized something momentous was about to occur. He pressed against her, his little hand curling in hers.

"I have come to tell you about your Christmas present," he announced to his children with a smile.

Sarah had never seen him smile before, and it startled her.

"A present?" Melissa demanded eagerly. "I love presents."

"Of course you do, my pet," her father teased. He sat down in a chair at the end of the table beside Alistair. "And you, son? Do you like presents?"

"Of course, Papa," the boy said courteously.

He is reserving judgement, thought Sarah. It was true that in the past several weeks, Mr. Whitfield had spent some time with his children, at least the older two, taking them riding and inviting them to join him on several trips into town. She didn't know the reason for his change of behaviour, but she wholeheartedly approved.

"Good. I have decided—that is, I loved your mother very much," he muttered, his cheeks flushing. Before the children could respond, he hurried on. "But I realize the—I realize how much you miss her and need someone to take her place. So I have decided to wed."

The easy teasing tone had left his voice. He was stiff and formal, as if announcing a distasteful decision. Sarah eyed him curiously.

When his announcement was met with stark silence, he said testily, "I thought my decision would please you."

"But who, Papa?" Alistair asked, his eyes wide.

"I don't know," he replied, and seemed unaware of the strangeness of his response. Sarah fought to keep her mouth from dropping open.

"But, Papa," Melissa protested, "how can you know you will give us a mother if you don't know who it will be?"

The squire's lips firmed in irritation, and Sarah held her breath, hoping he would not hurt Melissa's feelings.

"I am having a house party. There will be several young ladies attending who might suit. That is why I am informing you of my plans." He turned from his children to Sarah. "I know the house party will disrupt your schedule, of course, but it is necessary."

Sarah blinked several times. "Why, no, Mr. Whitfield, I do not think it will. Your guests will all be adults, of course, and the children and I shall carry on as before."

One dark eyebrow rose as he said, "I see you have not taken my meaning, Miss Barnes."

She said nothing, sure he intended to explain.

"The very point of taking a second wife is to provide a mother for my children. I have no desire to remarry."

Sarah could believe his words. The servants frequently talked of his dedication to his dead wife's memory. One had only to look at him to see the grief in his eyes.

"But I still do not—"

"I know it is highly irregular," he continued, ignoring her words, "but I intend to select as a wife whomever my children would like best as a mother. Therefore, they must meet my guests, spend time with them. I shall expect you to supervise them."

Staring at him in disbelief, Sarah barely remembered to nod in agreement. The man's wits must be addled, she thought.

"You mean we get to choose our new mama?" Melissa squealed with delight.

"Within reason, child. You cannot expect me to marry Nanny Buckets, of course," he cautioned, the teasing returning to his voice.

Even Alistair burst into giggles at the picture his father had presented. Nanny Buckington, affectionately called Nanny Buckets, had been the squire's own nanny and now served his children. Her grey curls and rotund figure would make a startling contrast to Mr. Whitfield's lean handsomeness.

"Now," Mr. Whitfield continued as he set Melissa down in a chair beside him and stood, "you must remember not to discuss this matter outside the school-room. We do not want to offend the candidates. Ladies like to believe we men are swept off our feet by their beauty.'' His cynical smile did not register with the children, but Sarah took note of it.

"When will they arrive, sir?" Alistair asked. Sarah smiled as the child squared his shoulders at this new responsibility. He would be an admirable master one day, she knew, but she hoped he learned laughter as well as his letters before that day arrived.

"In two days, son, so be prepared to make your evaluations. They are only invited for a week. I could not bear too much merrymaking,'' he added somberly, schooling his features to conceal his own feelings.

Sarah felt a stirring of sympathy in her heart for the man, which surprised her. Her only emotion in regard to her employer until now had been irritation that he neglected his children.

"I had best be on my way. Jenkins is waiting for me in the stables. If there are questions, Miss Barnes, you will inform me, please," he ordered as he hurried from the room.

ANTHONY WHITFIELD strode down the stairs as if he were being chased. His interview with his children had gone well, he thought, considering the subject matter. They seemed pleased with his decision.

He stepped out into the courtyard and drew a deep breath of chilly winter air. Lord, he hoped so, at any rate. He certainly would not take on the burden of a second wife for his own sake.

When he had gone to the schoolroom two weeks ago, nudged by a guilty conscience because he had not checked to see if his choice of governess was appropriate in the four months since he'd hired her, he had been stunned—even distressed—by the conversation he'd overheard. He had neglected the children since Larissa's death. He did not deny it. But he could keep the pain at bay only if he pretended their life together had never been.

Alistair's words that day had shaken him. For his child to believe he did not care about him was an indictment he did not want to face. Now a sigh slipped from him.

"Mr. Whitfield?" Jenkins asked, startling his employer.

He was surprised to discover he'd reached the stables.

"May I have a word with you, sir? Miss Barnes has requested a change of mount. She has a light hand with the horses, but I didn't want to grant her request without your saying so."

"What has she been riding?"

"Lady, but she's only good at a walk now. Nothing compared to Feather."

"Feather? Isn't the mare a little too fresh for a governess?" Reconsidering his words, he hastily added, "I mean, does Miss Barnes have the experience to control Feather?"

"Aye, that she does. She be a fine horsewoman. And Master Alistair and Mistress Melissa are improving daily under her tutelage."

"Very well, Jenkins, I shall trust your judgement. However, send a groom with them in case she runs into difficulties." The head groomsman nodded. Anthony added, "We shall be having a number of guests next week. Take on additional help and hire more hacks from the neighbours to meet their needs."

"Aye. How many guests?"

"I believe ten. Several of them, however, are older ladies who will prefer a carriage ride to a gallop over the meadow." In inviting his prospective brides, he had had to include their chaperons, as well. How he hated the idea of doing the pretty for an entire week. He almost groaned aloud when he realized that, for him, those conditions would never end once he married again. A wife did not allow her husband to ignore her.

"I need Storm saddled at once. I want to—to ride to the north field and see how it fared in the recent storm." In truth, he wanted to ride away from his difficulties. But no horse, not even his beloved Storm, could run so fast.

He stood waiting for his orders to be carried out, impatiently tapping his boot on the cobblestone, his mind reviewing his meeting with his children. His groomsman's words about the governess suddenly struck him.

Miss Barnes was an excellent horsewoman? He tried to remember the interview he had conducted with so

little interest four months ago. He vaguely recalled a
dumpy, dowdy female, her hair covered by a boring
grey bonnet, her figure reminding him of Nanny
Buckets's. Only her voice had caught his attention, a
low, soothing song of bell-like tones. He had not even
seen her eyes, as she kept her gaze trained on her
hands, in mended grey gloves, clasped in her lap.

The voice was the same. Even today, when she was
taken by surprise, her tones had soothed him, lured
him, as a Lorelei would lure the sailors upon the rocks.
He shook himself away from such a comparison.

But today, he'd faced a different woman. She was
still dressed in sober grey, of course, but her hair was
no longer covered by a bonnet. The long plait hanging
down her back could be called brown, but Anthony
remembered a hint of fire in it as she cuddled his
youngest son.

He could not remember asking her age during their
interview, nor her stating it. He had just assumed her
to be older. Now, as he remembered her fresh, blooming cheeks, he realized she could not have been long
from the schoolroom herself.

Her eyes were deep blue, staring up at him. And
damn it, her figure bore no resemblance to Nanny
Buckets's!

Why had she hoodwinked him? He had no doubt
that was what she had done, but he could not understand her reasoning. His musings were interrupted as
Jenkins reappeared, leading Storm.

"Jenkins, Miss Barnes, has she—that is, does she conduct herself as she ought?"

The man stared at him in surprise. "Miss Barnes, sir? Oh, aye, she's all right and proper, except with the little 'uns, a'course."

"What do you mean?"

"Why, she just loves them, you know. Even Master Alistair, as solemn as he is, gives a smile for Miss Barnes." The warmth in Jenkins's voice reassured Anthony. He had great respect for the man's judgement.

"But she is properly behaved with the staff?"

"A'course. She's a lady." He left no room for argument.

"Very well, thank you." Anthony swung into the saddle with practiced grace. "Send word to the house that I shall take my luncheon at the inn near Gablewood." With a wave of his hand, he urged the stallion out of the stable yard. He needed a few moments' forgetfulness of his children, his unknown future wife and, surprisingly, his puzzling governess.

He returned four hours later, having tried to come to terms with his plans for the future. His parents had died before he married. With Larissa he had found happiness and buried the pain of losing his family. When fate dealt him the additional blow of Larissa's death, he had decided to withdraw from life, from any more pain, vowing never to love again.

Unfortunately, he had selfishly forgotten his children. He'd been so horror-stricken when he overheard Alistair's words, he had committed himself to a second marriage. As much as he hated the thought of a new wife replacing Larissa, he wanted to compensate for his treatment of his children.

When he entered the house, he discovered that his plan was a little more complicated than he had first thought. His housekeeper, wife of Clayton, his butler, was wringing her hands near the back stairway when he emerged on the first floor. Listening to her was the mysterious governess.

"What's the matter, Mrs. Clayton?" he asked, but his gaze roamed over the governess. She definitely did not resemble Nanny Buckets, he decided, as her gown revealed a delicious roundness in certain areas, accentuating a surprisingly small waist. His housekeeper's complaint drew his reluctant attention.

"Mr. Whitfield, sir, it's been almost two years since we've entertained. I don't have the staff for a house party of this size."

"Then hire more help. Baxter will not refuse your requests," he said. His steward, after all, was in charge of the estate expenditures.

"A'course he wouldn't, sir, but I don't see how I can train them in such a short time."

"Well, you will just have to manage it, Mrs. Clayton. The invitations have already been sent."

His impatience grew as the woman appeared on the verge of hysteria. It was bad enough that he would have to suffer through the week. Must his staff make such a fuss over it?

"If I might make a suggestion?" Those lyrical tones he remembered so well drew both his and Mrs. Clayton's attention.

"Well?" He refused to be charmed.

"I thought perhaps if you asked your neighbours, they might lend you several trained members of their own staffs? Particularly if you intend to invite their employers to some of your entertainments." She added to Mrs. Clayton, "I'm sure you could hire housemaids and footmen to train for the future, and they could do the less skilled tasks now."

Mrs. Clayton appeared well pleased with the suggestion. Anthony, however, growled, "What entertainments?"

Both ladies stared at him as if he'd grown two heads. Finally, the governess ventured, "You surely have planned entertainments for your guests, Mr. Whitfield? Parties, rides, even picnics if the weather permits?"

He felt himself sinking in a morass of details he had hoped to avoid. "I—I assumed they would ride occasionally. I asked Jenkins this morning to obtain more mounts. *He* did not foresee a problem." He was even more annoyed to see Miss Barnes bite her full bottom lip in an unsuccessful attempt to hold back a smile.

"Well, a'course not," Mrs. Clayton protested. "Horses is easier than people."

He could not disagree with that assessment. In fact, given the choice, he would have returned to the stables and remained there until his guests had all departed.

"I shall be glad to offer my services to Mrs. Clayton if you like, Mr. Whitfield. I have . . . a little knowledge of the types of entertainment Quality enjoy, unless you have some preferences?"

"No, none at all. Very well, thank you, Miss Barnes. You and Mrs. Clayton arrange what you will. See Baxter if you have need of funds. I shall instruct him to accommodate you." With a brief nod, he strode away from the two women, relieved to have the difficulty solved.

He was still within earshot, however, when Mrs. Clayton declared in ringing tones, "Well, I never! That man is all about in the head!"

CHAPTER TWO

As WILLING as Anthony was to turn over to others the preparations for his house party, he found himself consulted at every turn. Oddly, however, Miss Barnes was not among those who approached him. Mrs. Clayton or her husband acted as her emissaries.

He assured himself he had no desire to see his children's governess. Nevertheless, the contrast of his earlier memories of Miss Barnes and his most recent observations intrigued him.

The afternoon before his guests' arrival, Miss Barnes herself finally knocked on the library door.

"Sir, if I might have a moment of your time?" she asked.

"Of course, Miss Barnes," he replied, his gaze noting her demure grey gown, her long plait of auburn hair wound in a simple coronet atop her head. Dark lashes shadowed her cheeks as she examined several papers in her hands.

"I have assigned rooms by order of importance of your guests, but I thought your personal interests might dictate a change in my planning."

She slid the papers before him, and he studied the neat lettering. "I have no difficulty with your assignments," he said briefly and returned the papers to her.

"But, Mr. Whitfield, the three young ladies are of equal rank, so I assigned their rooms randomly. Have you a preference? The green chamber is far superior to the others."

"No."

His brief reply had shocked her if he was to judge by the wide blue eyes trained on him. Finally, she shrugged and turned to leave. "Miss Barnes," he said, halting her exit, "forgive my impertinence, but...but has your person changed since our first interview?"

He watched in amazement as her cheeks flushed a becoming rose and her lashes dropped to hide her gaze from him.

When she said nothing, he added, "I do not recall our interview with any great clarity, but I had the impression of an older, more, uh, substantial person." Her bottom lip trembled as she murmured, "The agency would not offer employment to me because I was too young and, er..." She blushed even more.

Once again his gaze roved over her trim figure, its curves defined by her attire. Looking at his clasped hands on the desk, he said, "Ah, that explains my confusion. You employed a disguise. Most count beauty as an asset in this world."

Though she did not look at him, she said firmly, "Not in a governess, sir, unless the men in the family have dishonourable intentions towards her."

"I hope I do not have to assure you that such charades are not necessary here?"

"No, sir," she murmured, dropped a slight curtsy and hurried to the door.

Before she could leave, he called to her. "One moment, please. I wondered if you would explain your knowledge of entertainments. It seems rare in a governess."

She kept her gaze on the floor but her musical tones were clear. "My father was a clergyman, sir, and as such, he and his family were invited to many local events. In addition, I was given a Season in Brighton."

"Ah. To find a husband?" She nodded but offered no explanation. She had had no success or she wouldn't be employed as his governess, but he could see no reason in her appearance for such failure. In fact, she was more beautiful than most of the débutantes in London.

She stood waiting to be dismissed. He finally murmured, "Thank you for your efforts on my behalf." With another nod, she hurried from the room, rightly interpreting his remark as a dismissal.

When the door had closed behind her, Anthony leaned back in his chair. He could understand her use of a disguise. Miss Barnes, even clad in dull grey, would not be overlooked by any man if he had an interest in that direction. In spite of her demure behaviour, her figure would tempt many a man to abuse his authority over her.

Not him, of course. He was an honourable man. Besides, he was not drawn to any woman, not even the three he was considering as his future bride. His heart had lost interest in the distaff side when Larissa died.

No, Miss Barnes was safe in his household. She was fortunate to have landed here, where he devoted his time to managing his estate, because she was certainly a comely woman. Yes, a most enchanting young lady. But, of course, he had no interest in her.

SARAH HURRIED AWAY from the library, wishing to put distance between herself and that embarrassing interview. Mr. Whitfield need not have assured her he had no interest in her person. Because she had seldom seen him since her arrival four months ago, that was a natural assumption.

What a strange man! Not because he had ignored her existence, but because he appeared equally uninterested in the three ladies he contemplated marrying.

Furthermore, to offer to one's children the choice of his bride was unheard of. For a man who had avoided his children for four months—and probably longer—his parental sacrifice seemed decidedly odd. She sighed as she hurried back to the schoolroom. The children had been all atwitter since their father's visit.

Every day, in place of their studies, they wanted to discuss the qualities they sought in their future mother. She had grown weary of the subject after the first day, but Alistair and Melissa remained enthralled with the topic. She squared her shoulders and prepared to listen to their latest speculations.

"WHAT IF they're all horrible?" Melissa whispered to her brother. They were supposed to be napping on little cots at the far end of the schoolroom while Miss Barnes organized their father's party.

"Father wouldn't choose horrible ladies," Alistair assured his little sister, and only hoped he was right. On the few occasions they had met ladies when they went to town with their father, the women had seemed horrible to him, all concerned with their gowns or making a fuss over his father.

"I wish they would be like Miss Barnes," Melissa whispered. "I love her."

"Me too."

After several minutes of silence, Melissa asked, "Why can't Papa marry Miss Barnes? Instead of the other ladies?"

"Don't be silly, Melissa. He said he couldn't marry her."

"When did he say that?" Melissa demanded, popping up in her bed.

"Well, he said he wouldn't marry Nanny Buckets. It's almost the same thing."

"Is not! Miss Barnes is lots prettier . . . and younger, too."

"Yes, but he said we had to choose one of the ladies he's invited." Alistair frowned, trying to recall his father's exact words.

"Well, I won't like them! And I'll tell Papa so. He won't marry them if I don't like them."

"Then you won't have a mama for Christmas."

"Will, too! 'Cause I wished it on the Christmas Angel, just like Miss Barnes said!"

Melissa pressed her lips together in a stubborn gesture that was quite familiar to Alistair. He suppressed a groan. "The Christmas Angel can't make wishes come true, Melissa. That's just a story."

Melissa shot him a burning glare and jumped from her bed to race across the schoolroom.

"Where are you going?" Alistair whispered hoarsely, hoping not to rouse Nanny Buckets from her nap in the next room. His sister didn't answer, but she opened the door to Miss Barnes's bedchamber and slipped inside. Alistair sat up, debating whether to follow his sister or remain where he belonged. Before he came to a decision, Melissa returned with the dolly he'd found in the governess's room.

"You shouldn't take Miss Barnes's dolly!" he protested.

"I'm just borrowing it." She sat down on the edge of her brother's cot. "Look at her, Alistair. Isn't she beautiful? Just like a real angel. If you look into her eyes and make a wish, it will come true. I just know it!"

In spite of his stubborn practicality, the boy looked into the blue glass eyes and found himself accepting his sister's words. "Maybe," he whispered. "Her eyes are the same colour as Miss Barnes's eyes."

"I'm going to wish for Miss Barnes to be our mama. And I'm not going to like any of those other ladies." Melissa nudged him with her elbow. "Promise you won't, either."

Reluctantly, he nodded. "All right, I promise. But Papa's not going to be happy with us."

"He doesn't care which lady he marries, so he should please *us.*"

Both children stared at the china doll in Melissa's hand and prayed she was right.

EVEN THOUGH the guests would not arrive until afternoon, the entire household was tense with anticipation as soon as the sun rose the next day. Sarah did what she could to calm both Mrs. Clayton and her two charges, but her efforts were futile.

The third time she discovered Melissa at the window, watching for arrivals when she was supposed to be resting, Sarah abandoned the idea of a nap. "You may watch out the window, but do not wave or call out to your father's guests. That would be improper behaviour."

"We won't, I promise," Alistair said as he rushed across the room to his more adventurous sister.

"Your father wants you to join the guests for tea this afternoon after they have settled in. I shall help you dress."

"Must we go down?" Alistair asked, surprising Sarah.

"Yes, you must. Anyway, I thought you were anxious to meet your father's choices?"

"We won't like them," Melissa assured her firmly.

"How do you know until you meet them?" Sarah frowned as she watched Alistair elbow his sister.

"Melissa means she's *afraid* she won't like them."

"I see. Your father has been very generous in allowing you to choose your future mother. I believe you must come down to tea." She kept her voice firm, allowing no disagreement. She had enough to do today without spending time convincing the squire's children they must follow his orders.

"Yes, Miss Barnes," the children said at once, their angelic response somehow leaving more questions than answers.

Sarah was reminded of their surprising reluctance that afternoon as she approached the front parlour holding their hands. Alistair's grip tightened and Melissa tugged on Sarah's hand.

"Have you seen them?" she whispered.

"No, darling, I haven't. Mrs. Clayton showed them to their chambers. I'm sure they're very nice, however."

"One had a big bonnet. We could not see her face," Melissa said.

Clayton appeared at that moment to open the door to the parlour. Sarah bent down to the two children. "Be sure to mind your manners. Your father is counting on you."

They nodded gravely, apprehension in their gazes. Sarah released their hands and stood up. After a nod from her, Clayton opened the door to the parlour and the trio entered, Sarah gently prodding the children with a hand on their shoulders.

Sarah, too, was eager to see the candidates for the position of Mrs. Whitfield. After all, the woman chosen would be her future employer. And she might take a greater interest in the children's education than her husband.

The room seemed amazingly full of people. As Sarah and the children entered, the conversations stopped and everyone turned to stare at them. Alistair and Melissa instinctively moved closer to her.

"Ah, my children. May I present Master Alistair Whitfield and his sister, Melissa," Squire Whitfield said, advancing toward them.

Alistair gave a stiff bow as Sarah had coached him, and Melissa curtsied, sweeping her long lashes up to smile winsomely at her audience.

Laughter greeted Melissa's performance, and her smile broadened. Poor Alistair, unsure of the reason for the laughter, reddened and looked up at Sarah. She smiled to reassure him.

"And their governess, Miss Barnes," Mr. Whitfield added, surprising Sarah. She nodded and looked at each of his guests as he introduced them.

"May I present Lord Abbott and Mr. Crutcher, old friends of mine. Here is Mr. Denison and his daugh-

ter, Miss Denison, Mr. and Mrs. Myerson and Miss
Myerson, and Mr. and Mrs. Scott and Miss Scott.''

The introductions came so quickly that Sarah
scarcely had time to identify the guests. However, she
realized one guest was not present. Mr. Denison's wife
had been included in the invitation. Immediately, her
mind began to deal with seating at the dinner table. The
missing Mrs. Denison threw off her careful planning.

The parlour door opened to a parade of footmen
bearing trays of food, supervised by Clayton. Their
livery had been hastily assembled, but Sarah thought
they were presentable. At least Mrs. Clayton didn't
have to worry about clumsiness. The neighbours had
been delighted to offer the use of their best servants. It
had been several years since the squire had entertained, and they all looked forward to being included.

''Please be seated, Miss Barnes, and pour the tea for
us, if you will.''

Sarah swung round, startled at this new duty thrust
upon her, and stared at her employer. His firm nod
underlined his order.

She had assumed he would choose one of the older
ladies to play hostess. It would have been for the best,
assuming he alternated the duty among the guests until he'd made his decision in regard to his future wife.

With Alistair at her side, Sarah settled on the sofa
behind the table holding the tea tray. As the daughter
of a clergyman, she'd dispensed tea to larger gather-
ings than this one, so she felt reasonably composed, if
somewhat surprised.

"Alistair, would you please take this cup to one of the ladies?" she asked, smiling at the boy.

Mr. Whitfield frowned and started to speak, but she stared at him. Both of them held their breath as Alistair delivered his precious burden. The smile he gave Sarah when he had accomplished his task was well worth the suspense. She handed him another and began the process all over again.

Melissa left her father's side to come to Sarah. "I want to help, too."

"You may pass the sandwiches, Melissa." She handed the child a silver tray, showing her how to hold it with both hands. "How charming," Miss Denison cried as Alistair handed her her tea.

"Oh, yes," the other two young ladies agreed quickly, not to be outdone.

"And I do admire the furnishings in your parlour, Mr. Whitfield," Miss Myerson hurriedly added after a nudge from her mother, seated beside her.

"Thank you. My wife chose the furnishings."

"And how is that new breed of draught-horse working out?" Lord Abbott asked quickly, to Sarah's relief. She did not think a discussion of Mr. Whitfield's dead wife would be conducive to courting.

"Very well. I cannot wait to show you, John," Mr. Whitfield replied enthusiastically, turning his attention away from the ladies. Several of the other gentlemen knew nothing about his horses and were interested enough to ask questions, so that they all gravitated to one end of the room.

Mrs. Myerson turned to Sarah.

"How long have you been employed as governess here?" she asked. Though her question was all that was polite, the emphasis she placed on the word *employed* told Sarah of the woman's opinion of her presence in the drawing room.

"Four months, Mrs. Myerson."

"And how do you find Mr. Whitfield as an employer?"

"He is a fair and generous man. And his children are wonderful," she added with a smile at her charges.

"I adore children," Miss Scott said, a lisp enhancing the childlike quality of her voice.

"My daughter not only enjoys children, but she is also quite adept at disciplining them," Mrs. Myerson said.

Sarah hid a smile as Alistair and Melissa exchanged horrified looks. While Mrs. Myerson thought she was helping her daughter's cause, Sarah felt certain that the children had just crossed the young woman off their list.

"I think children should be loved," Miss Denison inserted with a lovely smile. A touching sentiment, Sarah thought, if only the young lady had not drawn back her skirts every time Alistair or Melissa had approached her.

"Pardon me, Miss Denison, but did your mother not accompany you and your father?" Sarah asked, still wondering about the number of guests.

"No, Miss Barnes. She grew ill at the last moment. Since we had already accepted the invitation, she insisted Papa and I come so Mr. Whitfield would not be disappointed." She patted her blond hair with a smile. "After all, it is not my mama he so particularly wanted to see."

Mrs. Scott leaned forward. "My dear Miss Denison, surely you don't believe—that is, Mr. Whitfield is quite partial to my Alberta." That young lady's cheeks glowed bright red, but she smiled in certain agreement.

Sarah looked at Mrs. Myerson, knowing that august woman would not allow such assumptions to go unchallenged. The woman surprised her, however.

"I'm sure Mr. Whitfield simply missed Town life and wanted a pleasant week with friends. After all, he is not the only eligible man here, you know. Lord Abbott and Mr. Crutcher are quite well thought of in Society."

Sarah blessed the woman, whatever her intentions. Her words effectively dampened the others' assumptions.

"As I've told my Frances," Mrs. Myerson continued, losing Sarah's goodwill, "an invitation to visit a man's home is not a marriage proposal, no matter how much partiality he has shown her."

"Would anyone care for more tea?" Sarah asked hastily. "Alistair, would you offer the ladies one of Cook's tea cakes? They really are splendid."

For the next few minutes, Sarah tried to keep the conversation centred on the children, the refreshments or Mr. Whitfield's holdings. The latter topic held the most interest for the ladies, but at least they were no longer sparring over Mr. Whitfield's preference in his guests.

Which was a good thing, Sarah decided with irritation, since the man had ignored all three ladies ever since Lord Abbott introduced the topic of horses. Realizing he would never remember to release his guests in time for them to rest before dressing for dinner, she excused herself to the ladies and crossed the room.

"Mr. Whitfield?"

He stopped in midsentence and stared at her—as if he'd never seen her before, she thought resentfully.

"Sir, dinner will be served in only two hours. I thought perhaps your guests might wish to retire for a brief rest before dressing for dinner."

He pulled out his watch and checked the time. "Surely you are not so tired, gentlemen?" he asked with a smile.

Sarah gritted her teeth, trying to maintain her smile. "The ladies might feel otherwise. Perhaps you could escort the gentlemen to the stables after the ladies retire."

"An excellent suggestion, Miss Barnes," he agreed, rising. With a bow in the direction of the ladies, he said, "We shall see you at dinner, ladies. Enjoy your rest." He executed a second bow and led the men from the room.

Mrs. Myerson raised her eyebrows in censure of his behaviour, and Sarah felt compelled to defend her employer. "Mr. Whitfield is a horse enthusiast, ladies. I fear that subject chases all else from his mind. May I escort you to your rooms?"

"Whitfield Manor is not so large that we cannot find our rooms, Miss Barnes," Mrs. Myerson assured her, her nose in the air. "Come, Frances."

The others followed in her footsteps, and soon only Alistair, Melissa and Sarah remained in the parlour.

"Now that we are alone, may I have another tea cake?" Alistair asked.

Sarah blinked several times before nodding. "Yes, of course. You and Melissa did very well. Thank you for helping me serve tea."

"It was fun," Melissa assured her, nibbling on a tea cake herself.

Sarah could not resist asking the two children the question burning in her mind. "Which lady did you like the best?"

"None of them," Melissa said calmly, licking a dab of icing from her finger.

Sarah couldn't help agreeing with Melissa's wisdom, but she said, "Your father said you must choose one of them."

Alistair and Melissa exchanged a look that made Sarah curious, but before she could ask them its meaning, the door opened on their father.

"Oh, good, Miss Barnes you are still here. Mrs. Denison became ill and did not accompany her husband and daughter."

"Yes, I know."

"That makes our numbers uneven, so you must join us for dinner." He smiled that devastating smile he seemed to reserve for special occasions and left the room again. This time Sarah could not keep her jaw from dropping.

CHAPTER THREE

SARAH STARED at the open cupboard in despair. It should not matter, she reminded herself, but honesty forced her to admit her shortcoming. She was vain. At least to the point that she wished to dress well for dinner.

It was all the squire's fault. Never had she imagined that her attendance would be required at the evening entertainments. Drat Mrs. Denison!

With a sigh, she removed the only gown possible for the evening, a violet silk. The dress was five years old. The last time she'd worn it had not been a happy occasion. She had learned the ways of the world then, when her handsome beau had abandoned her for a young lady with warts and a large dowry.

She held up the garment before her and examined it critically. At least the style of high waistlines had not changed. If she added the white lace she'd saved from one of her mother's gowns to the neckline, perhaps it would disguise her lack of fashion.

An hour later, in spite of her excellent needlework, she knew she'd failed miserably. In contrast to the elegant young women she'd met earlier, she would appear dreadfully unfashionable.

"It will serve as a reminder of your place in the scheme of things," she muttered to her image in the looking glass. She was destined to love others' children. Never to have her own home, her own family.

"Enough of these maudlin thoughts. You are here to serve Mr. Whitfield."

With that stiff lecture still hanging in the air, Sarah swept from the room, her mother's favourite Harwich shawl wrapped around her shoulders.

She was the first to arrive in the parlour, as she had intended, and settled by the fire to await her employer's arrival. She wanted to ensure that he selected one of the two matrons to fill the role of hostess. It would never do for her to sit at the foot of the table.

"Why, Miss Barnes, you are most prompt," Mrs. Myerson said as she entered the room, followed by her husband and daughter. "I did not know you were to join us."

"Mr. Whitfield asked that I do so to keep the numbers even. I do not normally dine downstairs," Sarah calmly assured the older woman.

"Of course not. You do not mind surrendering your place by the fire to me, do you, my dear? I find these older homes quite draughty."

Though there was another seat opposite Sarah that boasted the same benefit of closeness to the fire, she realized it was not warmth that Mrs. Myerson was seeking but superiority. Without a word, she abandoned her comfortable position and moved to a chair distant from the hearth.

Mrs. Myerson directed her daughter to the other chair beside the fire and chatted to her family, purposely ignoring Sarah. The Scotts arrived, closely followed by Mr. and Miss Denison. Only the three bachelors were missing.

How like Mr. Whitfield, Sarah thought. *He is unused to playing the host. It is a good thing he is choosing a wife, because he needs guidance.*

When the three gentlemen finally arrived, they found the other guests gathered round the fire. Mr. Whitfield greeted them all. Then he said, "As soon as Miss Barnes joins us, we shall go in to dinner."

"I am here, sir."

He spun around at the quiet, melodious tones, to discover his children's governess sitting in a corner far away from the others.

"My dear Miss Barnes, you should have come closer to the fire. I fear you may catch a chill. The house is occasionally draughty, you know."

Anthony began to move across the room, assuming Miss Barnes to be shy, though she had shown no shyness to this point, when Mrs. Myerson stood.

"There is no need for her to change her place now, Mr. Whitfield, since we are going in to dinner. Will you lead us in? My Frances would delight in your escort."

Anthony frowned. He did not care for the woman's forwardness. He gave in to the impulse that seized him. "Why, no, I thought Lord Abbott would lead us in to dinner, since he outranks us all. John, would you take in Miss Denison?"

Though Lord Abbott appeared startled by his friend's question, he bowed gracefully before the young lady and extended his arm.

"Thomas, you may escort Miss Scott, and Mr. Denison, Miss Myerson. We'll allow the husbands to escort their wives."

"But whom shall you take in to dinner?" Mrs. Myerson demanded, her outrage apparent.

"Why, Miss Barnes, of course. It is the least I can do, since she has graciously joined us at my request."

Sarah bowed her head, hoping to contain the hysterical laughter that welled up within her.

The man had no idea how to go on. And she was going to pay for his outrageousness. Mrs. Myerson would not let her forget her unwanted triumph.

"Miss Barnes?"

She looked up to find the others leaving the room and her employer standing beside her, his hand extended. "Sir, you should not have abandoned the young ladies," she whispered as she stood.

One eyebrow rose in surprise, and Sarah thought he had never looked so handsome.

"But I have not. I am escorting the loveliest of them all." He took her hand as she extended it and carried it to his lips.

Sarah gasped, her cheeks flooding with colour. Then she looked down, unable to sustain his admiring look. The lilac colour of her dress resurrected painful memories that served to restore her common sense. She pressed her lips firmly together and placed her hand lightly on his crooked arm to follow the others in to dinner.

He was playing a game. She had best remember that. Men of his wealth dallied with governesses for only one reason.

The others were awaiting their host to sort out the seating arrangements. "We did not put out place cards, sir," Sarah whispered frantically. "You must direct the seating. Choose one of the matrons to act as hostess. Place Lord Abbott on her right."

"Ah. Forgive our informality, friends," Anthony called before he began to direct the seating as Sarah had recommended, with one exception. He led her down the table to its foot and held out the chair for her.

What was his intent? To find her poisoned in her bed on the morrow? Mrs. Myerson would find some painful way to do her some such damage if that woman's expression was any hint of her thoughts.

"Please, Mr. Whitfield—" Sarah began, panic in her voice.

"It is only fair, my dear. You have done the work of the hostess, so you should reap the rewards."

Another hysterical giggle rose in Sarah's throat. He thought he was rewarding her? The poor man knew nothing of women.

Accepting her fate, with a silent promise to have an interview with the man before the evening was over, Sarah sat down. Fortunately, Mrs. Myerson was farther up the table, closer to Mr. Whitfield, but none of the ladies looked upon Sarah with approval.

ANTHONY STARED down the table at his hostess. She was lovely, but so different from Larissa. He had not acted as host since his wife's death. He was finding it difficult to shake off the melancholy that always seized him when he thought of Larissa.

"Your hostess is charming, Tony, but do you think it wise to expose her to the anger of the other ladies?" John, Lord Abbott, asked quietly.

"What? You think the others are angry because she is sitting there?"

John chuckled. "Surely you have not withdrawn from the world so far as to forget human nature? Mrs. Myerson would gladly kill for Miss Barnes's seat. I suspect she was the reason Miss Barnes was banished from the fire in the parlour."

Anthony felt a flash of anger surging through him. "She will not slight anyone of my household. I think I made a mistake inviting her and her family."

"I think you made a mistake in several of your choices, myself and Thomas excluded, of course. Surely there were more congenial guests you could have invited."

Anthony kept his gaze fixed on Miss Barnes, watching as Thomas put her at her ease, while Mrs. Scott, on her left, ignored her. "Most assuredly. But my purpose was not to enliven the countryside. You know I am content here."

Lord Abbott's attention was demanded by Miss Denison, seated to his right, and Anthony turned to Miss Myerson.

"I hope you enjoy the country, Miss Myerson," he said politely.

"Of course, sir. The country is lovely, though, of course, I prefer the parties and excitement of London. I cannot bear being away from it for long." A guilty look crossed her face, and she frantically looked to see if her mother had overheard her remarks.

Had he not been a gentleman, Anthony would have laughed in her face. The poor child had just broken one of her mother's rules, he was sure, and eliminated herself from any possible consideration as his wife.

"I, of course, prefer the country and seldom go to London," he assured her.

"Oh, but you would go for the Season each year, of course. Mama said you had only been absent because of your wife's death. She said when you remarry, you will go often."

"No."

"But you were there last week."

"Yes, for a few days. I occasionally have business to conduct, but I do not remove my household. I would expect my wife to remain here and care for my children."

He felt a twinge of guilt as the young lady's cheeks paled. She looked ready to flee his presence. It wasn't that he would refuse his wife the treat of visiting London, if that was her wish. But he was seeking a wife who would be content in the country, as Larissa had been.

Miss Myerson turned to her father, and Anthony concentrated on his food.

"What did you do to that young lady?" John whispered.

"Nothing," Anthony assured him, but he couldn't hide the guilt of knowing he'd discomfited his dinner partner.

"You were about to tell me the reason for this house party," John reminded him, and waited expectantly.

Anthony's eyes returned to his temporary hostess. "I was reminded of my duties to my children. I am choosing a wife."

He could feel John's gaze on him, but he refused to look at him. Instead, he watched Miss Barnes politely include Mrs. Scott in her conversation with Thomas.

"Is that why you invited three young ladies, all blond?" John demanded, laughter in his voice. "My dear Tony, it is someone with Larissa's heart, not her hair, that you must seek."

Anthony looked at each of the young ladies and realized he had indeed unconsciously chosen three blondes. "I was in a hurry," he muttered.

"Ah, well, perhaps one of them is more like Larissa than you think," John consoled him before he returned his attention to his dinner companion.

Anthony had no such demands upon him. Miss Myerson obviously no longer had any desire to converse with him. He could not hold back a grin as he thought of Mrs. Myerson's consternation when she discovered her child had lost interest in the prize she was so earnestly pursuing on her daughter's behalf.

He probably should have taken more time to consider his situation, Anthony realized. He had dashed off to Town to discover a mother for his children with little or no thought to living with the woman as his wife. He had only wanted to give Alistair and Melissa their wish for Christmas. But Christmas was only one day of the year.

Then he would be faced with his new wife every day, every night. He almost groaned aloud. He had missed the warmth of a woman in his bed, the lovemaking he'd shared with his wife. He carefully studied the three young ladies he'd invited. They were all lovely, but they did not stir his senses. Why had he not seen that in London?

His gaze collided with that of Miss Barnes. There was a question in her eyes. He finally realized she was asking permission for the ladies to withdraw. He nodded slightly and she stood, asking that the gentlemen excuse them.

Once the ladies had withdrawn, he found himself eager to finish the brandy served to the gentlemen and join the distaff side again. He feared Miss Barnes might need his assistance.

SARAH ESCORTED the ladies back to the parlour and then excused herself for a moment. In truth, she had no reason to consult with Mrs. Clayton, but she did not want to remain in a room full of angry women.

"Mrs. Clayton, the meal was superb. And Clayton, the service was faultless. I am sure Mr. Whitfield will compliment you also." Particularly if she reminded him. "I do not know how it could have been improved."

"Thank you, Miss Barnes. That new sauce recipe you gave me was just the thing. We couldn't have done nearly so well without your guidance," Mrs. Clayton replied, pleased.

"Nonsense. Mr. Whitfield is fortunate to have such a capable staff. Clayton, the ladies are ready for tea. And when you bring in the tray, would you please place it before Mrs. Scott? She will serve as hostess."

"But Miss Barnes, Mr. Whitfield placed you in the hostess's chair at dinner. Are you sure?" Clayton asked.

"He did?" Mrs. Clayton demanded, surprise in her voice. "Well, I never."

"I believe he had a small disagreement with one of the matrons, Mrs. Clayton. It was of little or no significance." Sarah did not need talk in the kitchens as well as abovestairs. "Mrs. Scott, please, Clayton," she reminded him before leaving the kitchen. She had hoped to remain hidden until the gentlemen joined them and then to excuse herself completely.

She'd had her fill of society for one evening. The thought of an entire week of the house party depressed her. She would have preferred to remain in the schoolroom. Surely there must be someone in the neighbourhood who could fill in for the absent Mrs. Denison. She would ask Mr. Whitfield.

When she quietly requested Mrs. Scott to play hostess with the tea tray, that lady's demeanour thawed towards her slightly. Mrs. Myerson, however, continued to cast daggers at her with her eyes. The three younger ladies chatted quietly amongst themselves, ignoring both Sarah and their mothers.

It was just as well, Sarah thought. What would she have in common with them? Their futures would take widely divergent paths. Once she had believed she, too, could be courted, married, but no more.

She dismissed the ache in her heart. Alistair, Melissa and Justin were filling the void, showering her with affection. She was most fortunate and must not forget it. Once the bride had been chosen and the others departed, life would return to normal.

When Clayton presented the tea tray to Mrs. Scott, Mrs. Myerson sat bolt upright in her chair and glared at Sarah. If she could, Sarah would have assured her that tomorrow night she would have the honour of dispensing tea, but it was impossible. Mrs. Myerson would not be mollified.

After all the ladies except Sarah had received a cup of tea, the gentlemen entered the room.

"We did not expect you to join us so soon," Mrs. Myerson cooed. "You could not stay away from such beauty, I see."

Sarah hid her smile. Such heavy-handedness would not sit well with Mr. Whitfield. She watched his eyes narrow even as he smiled in acknowledgement.

"I think it was the tea that drew us," he joked. "I would take a cup if all the ladies have been served, Mrs. Scott," he said, his eyes travelling round the room. He stopped short just as he was about to receive the cup of tea his guest extended.

"Miss Barnes, you have not received any tea? Forgive me. I shall serve you personally." Before Sarah could protest, he provided her with his cup of tea, received another from Mrs. Scott and pulled a distant chair beside her.

"You have no objection to my joining you?" he asked politely even as he sat down.

"Mr. Whitfield," she whispered, "are you trying to create enemies for me? Please go and talk to the young ladies."

"There is no room there."

"Lord Abbott managed to find a place next to Miss Denison."

"True. But he has always been swifter at such things than I. He is quite the polished gentleman."

"Perhaps the seat on the other side of Mrs. Scott?"

"You want me to flirt with a married woman? Shame on you, Miss Barnes. I did not know you were so liberal in your views."

Sarah could not keep the blood from rushing into her cheeks at his ridiculous teasing. A sharp glare from Mrs. Myerson reminded her of her duty, however.

"Sir, you must court the young lady you intend to marry. Perhaps Miss Myerson. She is lovely."

"Miss Myerson dislikes the country. She told me so quite plainly once her mother was not within hearing."

"Oh, surely she said no such thing."

He grinned. "Just think how dismayed Mrs. Myerson will be when she discovers that her only child has no desire to become Mrs. Whitfield."

Sarah tried to stifle her laughter at the wicked glint in his eyes, but she could not swallow all of it.

"You have said something amusing?" Mrs. Myerson demanded, her eyes never having left them since Mr. Whitfield joined the governess.

Afraid of what her employer would say if left to respond, Sarah hurriedly explained, "He was only telling me about one of the children on the estate, Mrs. Myerson. Mr. Whitfield takes a great interest in those who live here at Whitfield."

"Yes. So I see." The implication in the woman's voice was lost on no one as she glared at the pair of them.

Sarah felt her cheeks flooding with colour again. She had never blushed so much in one evening. Mr. Whitfield stiffened beside her and she feared his response. She was discovering her employer had a temper.

Lord Abbott responded before the squire could do so. "Indeed, Anthony is an exemplary owner. That is why his home farm is so prosperous, as well as his stables. Did your husband tell you of Anthony's success at the races?''

"I do not hold with gambling," Mrs. Myerson said stiffly, and Sarah almost burst into laughter again as Mr. Myerson looked guilty. The poor man, as well as his daughter, must be ruled by his autocratic wife.

"I agree, Mrs. Myerson," Anthony said, surprising that lady. "I race my horses to show the world their strength, endurance and speed. It is a business, you see. Because my horses do well at the races, they bring a high price on the market."

"Mama says it is better for men to spend their time at the race track than—'' Miss Denison halted abruptly, her cheeks flaming when she realized not all her mama's pearls of wisdom were acceptable in mixed company.

Lord Abbott, always the gentleman, rushed to her rescue. "Than in their clubs drinking. Too much wine is not healthy," he assured the company, even as he patted Miss Denison's hand.

Mr. Denison hurried to assist the other's gallantry. "My wife has never objected to my attending the races. She even accompanies me on occasion. She is most knowledgeable about horses."

The conversation continued on the topic of horses until it, too, was exhausted, and there was a general move to retire.

Sarah hung back, hoping to have a brief conference with Mr. Whitfield. When only he and his two friends remained, she spoke.

"Sir, might I have a moment of your time before you join your friends in the billiard room?"

The other two, after offering good-nights, strolled from the room, leaving Sarah alone with her employer.

CHAPTER FOUR

ALL THE THINGS Sarah had wanted to speak to Mr. Whitfield about disappeared from her head when she found herself alone with him, his grey eyes trained on her face.

"I—I wanted to say—that is, please do not have me as hostess again. Your guests—the other ladies do not approve."

"It is not their right to approve my hostess," he assured her, a glint of anger in his eyes.

He had the look of a warrior off to battle, and a vision of him in knight's armour facing Mrs. Myerson, who, of course, wore the suit of the black knight, brought a smile to her face. "Perhaps not, sir, but you have placed me in the unenviable position of being the object of Mrs. Myerson's malevolence."

Mr. Whitfield's features relaxed into a grin. "My apologies. Do you think we could rescind the Myersons' invitation since dear Miss Myerson has eliminated herself from the competition?"

"I believe not, Mr. Whitfield," Sarah said, still smiling. "Besides, I thought the children were to choose your bride?"

"Hmm, you have me there, Miss Barnes. Could you not drop a hint into their little ears that Miss Myerson does not care for the country and would be constantly in Town?"

"No, Mr. Whitfield. It is not my place to interfere in the children's choice."

"Naturally. I *would* choose a governess with a conscience." He shrugged his shoulders, still smiling. "By the way, Miss Barnes, you performed your unexpected duties admirably."

"Thank you, sir, but I should rather not do so again."

"Nor should I...entertain guests, that is," he added at her puzzled look. "But I'm afraid neither of us has a choice."

Sarah frowned. "But can you not alternate the duties of hostess between Mrs. Myerson and Mrs. Scott?"

"It would go against the grain to allow Mrs. Myerson to occupy such an important role, especially since there is no possibility of her daughter's becoming my bride. And I could not give the role solely to Mrs. Scott without increasing her expectations beyond belief." He waited, a small smile on his face, for her to dismiss his argument.

She could not.

"The rector's sister might agree to serve you."

"She might believe I had an interest in her if I asked her to act as my hostess."

Sarah pictured the elderly Miss Bonner, her prim lips stretched into a flirtatious smile, and choked on suppressed laughter. "Please, sir, do not make fun. There must be some solution."

"I can think of none without some lady's misconstruing my intent."

"And I shall do, as I am no lady," she muttered, the humour suddenly disappearing from their conversation. "I understand," she said more clearly and curtsied. But before she could speed from the room, as was her intent, a strong hand wrapped around her arm.

"Nay, Miss Barnes, do not search for the insult." He cocked his head slightly to meet her lowered gaze. "Not only are you a lovely lady, but you are also an excellent hostess. What's more important, you understand the circumstances. To whom else could I confide such a secret? Miss Bonner would think my wits had gone begging."

"Yes, sir," she whispered, the warmth of his touch spreading through her. When she did not lift her head, he raised it for her, his finger beneath her chin.

"Will you help me for my children's sake?"

"Yes, Mr. Whitfield."

"Thank you."

To Sarah's surprise, he bent and brushed his lips against her cheek. She gasped and pulled away.

As if unaware of her reaction, he stepped back and said matter-of-factly, "Now, what do we have planned for the morrow?"

She quickly gathered her wits about her. "We have an afternoon outing to choose a Christmas tree, as you requested, and greenery to decorate the house. I still do not understand about the tree.''

"Ah. When my wife and I travelled to Europe on our honeymoon, it was the Christmas season. In Germany we saw evergreens brought into the houses and decorated with bows and candles. Larissa insisted we do the same for our first Christmas here. It has been a tradition ever since.''

She nodded but looked away from the painful memories reflected in his eyes. ''Very well. I'll send one of the footmen to Town to purchase extra ribbon and candles.''

"And since there is no snow, we'll need carriages for the outing. Have you notified Jenkins?'' He turned and walked back toward the fireplace, putting distance between them, which allowed Sarah to breathe more easily.

"Yes, I have.''

"Very efficient, Miss Barnes. Is there anything I need to do?''

"I—I think it would be well received if you praised the Claytons for the food and the service at dinner this evening. Mrs. Clayton was nervous and—''

"Of course, you are right. Thank you for reminding me.''

There was a smile on his face again, which relieved Sarah, though she could not explain her concern for his happiness.

"I will say good-night, then,'' she murmured, and walked to the door. When he said nothing, she stopped and looked back at him as he gazed into the fire. "Good night, sir."

He turned then, a smile on his lips, "Good night, Miss Barnes. Sleep well."

ANTHONY HOPED his children's governess *would* sleep well. He would not. What had possessed him to kiss Miss Barnes? He had no interest in her—or in any woman, for that matter. The ladies invited to his manor house aroused no desire in him. They seemed little more than children, playing dress-up.

Miss Barnes, on the other hand, had unexpectedly filled the role of hostess with grace and intelligence. Gratitude. That was the reason for his behaviour. The softness of her skin, the blue of her eyes, her lingering scent had nothing to do with it.

Nothing at all.

He turned abruptly and strode from the room. Too much introspection was not good for a man. He broke stride to change direction and head for the servants' quarters. Better to talk to the Claytons now before they retired for the night.

When he finally joined his two friends in the billiards room, he discovered them discussing what he'd revealed to Lord Abbott at dinner.

"John says you intend to get leg-shackled," Thomas Crutcher said as soon as he entered. "Why? You have no need of heirs."

"No, only a mother," Anthony muttered, reaching for a billiard cue.

"You want a mother?"

"Don't be a clunch, Thomas. I need a mother for my children." He motioned for Lord Abbott to start the game.

"It's natural for a man to marry, Thomas," Lord Abbott said. "You should consider it."

"That's strange advice coming from a bachelor like you, John," Thomas complained.

"But I, too, am thinking of changing my marital state."

Both Thomas and Anthony froze in their tracks and stared at their friend. "You have never spoken of it before," Anthony finally said.

"I need an heir. My cousin died on the Continent, and now there is no one left but me." John made a shot and stepped back from the table to consider his next move.

"But if you marry, and Anthony takes another wife, I shall be left alone, an aging bachelor," Thomas protested. "I shall have to marry, also."

"That's what I suggested," John said as he bent for another shot. "There are three charming ladies here for the purpose of finding a husband. Why not just divide them up and be done with it?"

Thomas and Anthony exchanged stunned glances before Anthony protested. "Wait! I invited those three ladies for myself."

"Don't be greedy, Tony. You can't marry all three. Just tell us which one you are going to select."

"I wouldn't choose any of them, if you ask me," Thomas inserted.

"Why not?" John demanded, his casual air suddenly gone.

"Because the pick of the lot would be Miss Barnes. She's a looker, and has a pleasant way about her, besides."

"Miss Denison is an angel!" John retorted, his chin raised and his shoulders thrown back, as if waiting for a challenge.

Anthony eyed his two friends with surprise. After an awkward silence, he said, "If you have an interest in Miss Denison, John, I shall not stand in your way."

"What is the matter that *you* don't consider her?" he demanded.

Anthony held up his hands in surrender, a grin on his face. "Would you rather I announce my intent to wed her?"

After John apologized, Anthony continued, "There is nothing wrong with Miss Denison. Who can explain the ways of love? She does not stir my senses. I cannot explain why."

"You are sure?" John asked eagerly, the game forgotten as he walked towards Anthony. "I have been thinking of the necessity to marry for some time, but today, when I met Miss Denison, I—I just knew that she would be the perfect wife for me."

Anthony clapped his hand on Lord Abbott's shoulder. "Then I wish you well, my friend."

"I shall not speak yet. I don't want to frighten her," John said, his gaze unfocussed as he thought of his new love.

"Titles rarely frighten London misses," Thomas muttered, but John didn't hear him.

"And that still leaves you with two ladies to choose from," John added, looking at Anthony.

"Yes, of course," he agreed, but could summon little enthusiasm.

"I still think the best choice would be Miss Barnes."

Anthony whirled around to face his friend. "Miss Barnes is the governess to my children, Thomas. You will not speak of her in such terms again."

Thomas blinked. "I am not to say she is lovely?"

"No, of course not. She is indeed lovely. But she is not . . . she is to be treated with all due respect. She is assisting me in my search for a wife. That is all."

Thomas still appeared confused. "I meant no disrespect, Tony."

"I did not mean—" Anthony broke off, as confused as his friend. "Come, let us play and forget about ladies. I want no thought of brides to mar the rest of the evening."

Thomas readily agreed, but John's mind was solely on one particular bride. He did not show his customary skill that night.

And Anthony discovered that his earlier prediction of a restless night was realized.

"DID YOU NOT LIKE *ANY* of the ladies visiting your father?" Sarah asked the children the next morning. The sooner Mr. Whitfield made his choice, the sooner she would be excused from the unpleasant company of his guests.

Alistair looked up from his work and then tucked his chin into his chest and pretended not to have heard her question. Melissa, however, put down her pen and looked at Sarah.

"What did you think, Miss Barnes?"

"It is not my place to give an opinion, Melissa. Your father asked that you and Alistair choose his wife."

"What if we each choose a different one? Will Papa marry both of them?" Melissa asked with a giggle.

"No, of course not, dear. That's not . . . not acceptable. Your father will only marry one lady." And he did not even appear interested in one wife, much less two. Sarah sank her teeth into her bottom lip to quell the laughter. It was too bad she could not share Melissa's question with her employer.

"I am grateful for that, at least."

Sarah's head snapped up at the lazy baritone. Leaning against the open door was Mr. Whitfield. "Do not dare laugh, Miss Barnes."

His teasing grin almost broke her control, but she swallowed back her chuckles and said calmly, "Of course not, sir."

"Well, Melissa, Alistair, have you any preferences so far as to your new mama?" He strolled into the room and joined the trio at the small table where the children worked.

"No, Papa," Melissa chirped, a smile on her face. "They are all lovely, of course," she opined, sounding very grown-up, "but we do not yet know them."

"Ah, I see. Perhaps you will be able to visit with them this afternoon, when we go to the woods."

"Yes, I 'spect we will do so," Melissa said, nodding wisely, but there was an impish look in her eyes.

Sarah watched the two children, her curiosity roused. Melissa appeared to be harbouring a secret. Nor was Alistair being completely open. In fact, he was doing his best to disappear.

"Alistair," Mr. Whitfield prodded gently, "you have said nothing. Are you in agreement with your sister?"

"Yes, sir," he said without looking up.

"Do you think the ladies are pretty?" their father asked.

"Not as pretty as Miss Barnes," Alistair said in a rush, and then turned bright red.

"Thank you, Alistair," Sarah murmured, concerned for the child's embarrassment, though her own cheeks flamed, as well.

"You are right, of course," Anthony said, putting his hand on his son's shoulder and grinning at Sarah. "Shall I marry her?"

"Mr. Whitfield, you must not tease Alistair," Sarah chided. It was too bad of the man to tease both of them! "He is most gallant to compliment me so, but he, of course, knew you meant to discuss the three young ladies. Didn't you, Alistair?''

"Yes, Miss Barnes." Alistair concentrated fiercely on his lettering.

"Which of the ladies do *you* like, Papa?" Melissa asked, coming to Alistair's assistance.

"They are all charming."

"One talks funny, like Justin," Melissa noted. "And the lady in the purple gown seemed cross."

"Mrs. Myerson is already married, dear," Sarah explained as she exchanged a smile with Mr. Whitfield. "It is her daughter who is to be considered."

"But won't she be just like her mother?" Melissa asked.

Sarah opened her mouth to respond and then met the squire's glance again. She shrugged and left it to him to answer.

"An astute observation, child. I had no idea I had such a brilliant daughter," Anthony said with a grin. "That leaves only Miss Denison."

"She's very lovely," Sarah agreed.

"Yes, she is," Mr. Whitfield agreed, smiling.

Sarah turned away from his bright gaze, unwilling to admit to herself the sadness that stole into her heart at his words.

"But I 'spect we'll find something wrong with her, too," Melissa said.

"Why would you think that?" Sarah asked, drawn back to their conversation by Melissa's strange remark.

The child developed a sudden interest in her schoolwork, which made Sarah all the more suspicious. Picking up her pen, Melissa said, "Look, Papa. I'm doing nicely, don't you think?"

"Yes, indeed, my child. Well, the gentlemen are going to ride this morning, so I must descend to breakfast. All is under control, Miss Barnes?"

"Yes, of course, Mr. Whitfield," she assured him, her gaze roving over his manly form as he stood. When she realized she was recalling his gentle kiss and imagining his strong arms about her, drawing her into a more intimate embrace, a blush stole over her cheeks. She only hoped he could not read her thoughts. Still, she was strangely disappointed when he turned away.

"Good. Then I'll see you at luncheon," he said to his children. "After we eat you will be joining us for our trip to the woods. Dress warmly."

The children nodded and said goodbye to their father. All three watched the door until his footsteps could no longer be heard.

"What are you two hiding?" Sarah asked abruptly.

Alistair's eyes widened, horror on his face. Melissa eyed her governess calmly.

"Whatever do you mean, Miss Barnes?" she asked.

"I think you are planning something, or... or have not been honest with your father." Sarah looked at Alistair. "Were you honest, Alistair?"

"Yes, Miss Barnes," the boy assured her with ringing assurance. "I think you are the prettiest of all."

Sarah smiled reluctantly. "Oh, Alistair, darling, your father wanted to know only about the three ladies who are his guests. But thank you."

Melissa seemed quite content, but Sarah asked her, anyway. "And you, Melissa? Did you lie to your father?"

"No, Miss Barnes. One lady does talk funny. And we did not like Mrs. Myerson at all."

Sarah gave up. If the children would not tell her, there was little she could do but watch and wait.

"Very well. I need to confer with Mrs. Clayton about the luncheon. Please finish your letters while I am gone."

Both children bent over their slates with more than usual concentration, increasing Sarah's suspicion. She watched them for a moment and then left the room.

After several minutes, Melissa whispered, "Is she gone?"

"Yes," Alistair said quietly.

"We must plan."

"Plan what?" he asked, alarm in his voice, though he kept it low.

"Papa likes Miss Denison. We must find something wrong with her." Melissa wrinkled her little nose, lost in deep thought. "I cannot think of anything. Can you?"

Alistair shook his head miserably. He hated subterfuge. It made him feel guilty when he looked at Miss Barnes. "Why can't we just tell Papa the truth?"

"No, no, no, Alistair. You do not understand things at all."

"I do, too. I am older than you."

"I know, but...oh, never mind. I shall think of something."

That was what Alistair feared.

As ANTHONY LED his guests in pairs across the meadow, he watched Lord Abbott choose Mr. Denison as a riding partner. It appeared John was indeed serious in his pursuit of Miss Denison.

Which eliminated the last candidate, according to his children. Of course, they were not yet aware of that fact, but he wondered if they would be disappointed if he did not choose a bride, after all. Perhaps they would even be pleased, as they certainly did not appear enthusiastic about any of his guests.

Neither was he.

He chuckled as he thought of Alistair's response to his question. His son showed excellent taste in choosing Miss Barnes as the most beautiful. This morning, even in her plain gown, bent over the table, working with his children, she had appeared incredibly lovely and dewy fresh. And, he realized, warm and loving.

John's remark of last evening came back to him. He had tried to replace Larissa by choosing three blondes. But, as John said, he should have looked deeper. It was not blond hair that had made Larissa special.

His thoughts returned to Miss Barnes. She'd lived contentedly in the country for four months. In fact, he'd scarce been aware of her presence. Did she like the country? He realized he had no idea of his employee's preferences. Perhaps this afternoon he would ask questions of Miss Barnes while his children visited with his guests.

There was one thing he already knew about his children's governess, though he'd tried to deny it for days. Sarah Barnes had awakened a physical hunger in him that he'd thought he had buried with his wife.

He wanted to kiss her again.

CHAPTER FIVE

SARAH GAVE herself a stern lecture before she descended for luncheon. She'd had her heart broken once. That was enough. Even though she admitted to herself that she was attracted to Mr. Whitfield, to his unexpected sense of humour, his misplaced gallantry, and, yes, his handsome face, she must put such thoughts away.

In just a few days he would choose an appropriate bride.

Miss Denison.

"That is a lovely gown, Miss Denison," Sarah said with a smile after greeting the guests. In a day dress of pale pink lawn, the young lady did look fetching.

"Yes, a lovely gown," Mrs. Myerson agreed. "My own Frances goes to the same dressmaker. Isn't her gown stylish?"

Miss Myerson blushed as all eyes turned to her.

"Absolutely charming, ma'am," Sarah agreed. "In fact, you all appear to great advantage."

"Miss Barnes is correct," Anthony said, moving over to stand beside her. "Our ladies certainly brighten the room, don't they, gentlemen?"

There was general agreement, as Anthony expected, but he had effectively drawn the attention away from Miss Myerson. "Shall we go in to luncheon?"

Lord Abbott, who had placed himself next to Miss Denison, promptly extended his arm to her.

She blushed prettily and accepted his escort.

Sarah's gaze flew to Mr. Whitfield. "Sir," she whispered hurriedly, "should *you* not escort Miss Denison?"

"Why, no, I think not." He took her hand and drew it through his arm.

Mrs. Myerson glared at Sarah as if she had orchestrated Mr. Whitfield's movement. With a sigh, Sarah smiled at the woman and followed her companion's lead.

"Do you think she will poison your soup?" he whispered on the way to the dining hall.

"I shall not give her the opportunity," Sarah returned, smiling at his teasing. "Perhaps I should switch my bowl with yours, however—just to be safe."

"Unfortunately, we are at opposite ends of the table, Miss Barnes. Such a manoeuvre would be impossible." His smile was wickedly teasing.

Sarah withdrew her arm and sat down in the chair he held for her, hoping to steady her breathing. Suddenly she was grateful for the length of the table that separated them.

During the meal, she watched as Lord Abbott hung on Miss Denison's every word, while Mr. Whitfield only occasionally conversed with Miss Myerson, again on his left. Sarah resolved to assist Mr. Whitfield in becoming acquainted with Miss Denison during the afternoon excursion. Probably Lord Abbott had no idea of his friend's wish to spend time with that lady.

"I have dined here often the past two years," said Thomas Crutcher, seated beside Sarah, interrupting her thoughts. "The meals have greatly improved. Has Tony hired a new cook?"

Distracted, Sarah blinked several times before she comprehended his question. "Oh, no, sir. Mrs. Clayton is still in charge of the kitchens."

"Well, she has certainly improved her hand with the soup," he said, smililng at her.

"I shall tell her, Mr. Crutcher. She will be very pleased with your appreciation."

Anthony stared at his friend and Miss Barnes, wondering what subject held their attention. He hoped he did not need to warn Thomas again that Miss Barnes was not to be trifled with.

Perhaps he should reconsider Miss Barnes's suggestion to allow the two matrons to act as hostess. He did not want his children's governess to suffer from her duties.

Yes, he decided, feeling quite generous, he would ask Mrs. Myerson to play hostess this evening, and Mrs. Scott tomorrow. Of course, that would necessitate a rearrangement of the seating. But that mattered little compared to Miss Barnes's comfort. He would tell her immediately after luncheon.

At the end of the meal, Anthony stood. "I invite you all to join us in search of greenery for Christmas decorations. Perhaps even mistletoe to make a kissing bough." The gentlemen gave a cheer as several of the younger ladies blushed. "And a Christmas tree, a custom I brought back from Germany. Dress warmly and we shall prepare to leave in half an hour."

There was a buzz of excitement among the guests as they left the dining table. Sarah moved to Miss Denison's side.

"Will you accompany us, Miss Denison?"

"Oh, yes. I shall enjoy being outdoors," she replied, her eyes sparkling in anticipation.

"I'm glad," Sarah said, doing her best to admire the young lady. "Mr. Whitfield's children will come also. Would you care to ride in the carriage with them? They would enjoy your company."

"Why...why, yes, of course," Miss Denison agreed, though she cast a quick look over her shoulder at Lord Abbott.

"Wonderful. I shall tell them of the treat in store for them." With a smile, Sarah moved away from the other young lady, unsure how long she could maintain her cheerfulness.

With the intent of completing her plan, she drifted with apparent casualness to where Mr. Whitfield stood chatting with Mr. Scott. When that gentleman turned to go up the stairs, Sarah stepped closer to her employer. "Sir, the children asked if they might ride with you on our excursion this afternoon. They are a little shy among your guests."

"A capital idea, Miss Barnes," he readily agreed.

There was a warmth in his gaze that worried Sarah. She stepped back. "Thank you. I shall go and assist the children in their preparations." She hurried up the stairs, aware of his gaze on her. If her plan worked, perhaps Alistair and Melissa would approve their father's choice by this evening.

ANTHONY WAS PLEASED with Miss Barnes's suggestion. Suddenly he was looking forward to their outing. An afternoon spent with his children and their governess would be enjoyable.

"Have you looked outside?" Thomas asked, interrupting Anthony's thoughts.

"No. Why?"

"I think it will start snowing any minute. Are you sure the ladies will want to go out?"

"If not, they may stay by the fireside. But Miss Barnes needs the greenery to decorate the house."

"Miss Barnes is a handy female. She has certainly improved your kitchens, from all I can tell."

Anthony turned and stared at his friend. "Miss Barnes is quite efficient," he agreed, his voice brisk and businesslike.

"That's what I said."

"Go fetch your outer garments, Thomas. We shall leave shortly." With a shrug, his friend departed, and Anthony followed in his footsteps. Thomas's constant praise of Miss Barnes irritated him. Not that he didn't agree with his friend, but he did not like the attention he was giving the governess. It was not appropriate.

When he returned to the hall, three carriages were drawn up out front, although the two matrons chose to remain in the warmth. Anthony strode forward eagerly, searching for Miss Barnes. He discovered her standing outside by the open door of the first carriage, the hood of her cloak shielding her from the first falling flakes.

"Ah, Miss Barnes, prompt as usual. Are the children—"

"We're here, Papa!" Melissa called, darting her head out of the open door.

"I can see you are. I shall join you in just a moment, as soon as the others are ready. Stay inside where it is warmer."

Melissa subsided back into the shadowy interior, and he turned to the governess. The dark grey of her hood contrasted with the auburn hair framing her face.

"You should get inside also, Miss Barnes. There is no need to freeze yourself. I shall just see to the others."

Assuming her obedience, Anthony began to lead the others to the carriages.

Sarah waited until his back was turned before scooting past him and greeting Miss Denison at the door.

"The children are waiting for you, Miss Denison. Come this way." She took the young lady's arm and led her to the first carriage.

"Is Lord Abbott joining us?"

"Lord Abbott?" Sarah repeated, feigning innocence, "No, I do not think so. The carriage would be too crowded." She motioned for the footman to assist Miss Denison into the vehicle and closed the door.

Lord Abbott came down the steps at just that moment. While Mr. Whitfield assisted Miss Scott and her father into the second carriage, Sarah met him and indicated the third carriage.

"If you do not mind, I shall join you and Mr. Denison," she added as they approached the carriage. As a gentleman, of course, Lord Abbott could not protest.

"And perhaps Miss Denison might want to ride with us, also?" he asked, looking around.

"Oh, she has already joined Mr. Whitfield and his children. She is a great favourite with his children, you know," Sarah assured him with a smile pasted on her lips.

She greeted Mr. Denison, already snugly seated inside under several fur rugs, with his feet on a pan of hot coals. As soon as Mr. Crutcher joined them, the carriages set out. Sarah began to speak of Miss Denison's attributes and how impressed Mr. Whitfield and his children were with her.

Mr. Denison seemed quite pleased with her conversation, but Lord Abbott grew more and more withdrawn. Sarah felt cruel to dash his hopes so thoroughly, but after all, Mr. Whitfield had chosen Miss Denison first. It really was unfair of Lord Abbott to try to sway her interest.

"WE ARE OFF," Anthony called gaily as he swung into the carriage. After closing the door and sitting back, he turned to the lady beside him. "Are you warm...Miss Denison? I thought you were in the other carriage with Lord Abbott."

His children, seated across from them, stared at him, wide-eyed. Miss Denison, too, watched him.

Finally, she said, "Miss Barnes said you and your children would like me to ride with you."

"Of course we are pleased to have you with us." After an awkward pause, he said, "Do you like snow? I fear we may see a lot of it before we return to the house." He pictured again the scene in front of the house, certain he'd left Miss Barnes standing beside his carriage. Where had she gone?

When he saw the skirts of a lady entering the third carriage, he'd assumed it was Miss Denison joining her father and Lord Abbott. But he'd been wrong. Or perhaps Miss Barnes had not come, after all.

No, she would not abandon the outing. After all, she was responsible for the children. If he had learned anything at all about Miss Barnes, it was that she did not shirk her duty.

"Well, we shall be able to show Miss Denison how beautiful our land is, shan't we, children?" he said, hoping to elicit some response from his silent off-spring.

"Yes, Papa," Alistair finally said when his father stared at him. Melissa was playing with her mittens.

"Are you warm enough, Melissa?"

"Yes, Papa."

"Miss Denison, do you enjoy the country?"

"Oh, yes, Mr. Whitfield, though I enjoy Town also. But I would not want to spend Christmas in the city. Christmas is special." The glow in her eyes appeared to awaken a response in his children.

"Yes, Christmas is a magic time," Melissa agreed. "Do you have a Christmas Angel?"

Miss Denison appeared surprised, but she responded, "Yes, of course. There is an angel that goes above the crèche. You must have a crèche also."

"Not that kind of angel," Melissa said, shaking her head. "I mean—"

"Melissa," Alistair said urgently, "look, the snow is coming down faster."

Anthony watched his children, puzzled. He knew Melissa was referring to Miss Barnes's dolly, but he didn't understand why Alistair did not want to tell Miss Denison of it.

"But, Alistair—"

"We may be able to build a snowman when we return. May we, Papa?"

"Perhaps, if it is not too cold. Have you ever built a snowman, Miss Denison?"

"Oh, yes, when I was younger. I would love to assist in the building of your snowman, Alistair, if I may."

Alistair stared glumly at the lovely lady beside his father. "Yes, of course, if it is not too cold."

Why, Anthony wondered, did the idea of building a snowman with Miss Denison distress his son so? Melissa, too, looked unhappy. It was a relief when the carriage stopped, signalling they had arrived.

As they descended from the carriages, they realized the snowstorm was in earnest. Huge white flakes dashed down in profusion, coating everything with a soft glowing of white. By the time Anthony had assisted the children and Miss Denison to the ground, he discovered Miss Barnes waiting for Alistair and Melissa.

"I thought you were to accompany us, Miss Barnes," he said in a low voice as Miss Denison searched the area, her hand shielding her eyes, as if seeking something she'd lost.

"I feared your carriage would be too crowded. Did the children behave themselves?" Sarah asked, keeping her attention on her charges.

"Of course, though they do not seem particularly happy. Even the idea of building a snowman did not entice a smile to Alistair's lips." He noticed Miss Barnes did not seem any more cheerful than his son.

"Perhaps he is nervous." She turned from him to his son. "Alistair, shall we search for the perfect tree?"

When she extended her hand, Alistair brightened at once.

"Oh, yes, Miss Barnes. We must choose it carefully."

Before Anthony could protest, both children had seized Miss Barnes's gloved hands and left him standing alone with Miss Denison.

He suddenly realized Lord Abbott had not appeared at the young lady's side, and he, too, looked round. "There is John, assisting the servants in building a fire. Why don't we move closer? I'm sure you will be grateful for the warmth."

"It...it is rather cold," she responded with a shiver.

He led Miss Denison over to the clearing near the road where the coachmen were gathering wood. Soon, the wood was lit and the first small flames began to spread.

"Well done, men," Anthony said. "Thanks for your help, John," he added, turning to his friend. "I have brought Miss Denison to the fire. It is chillier than I thought."

"Miss Denison," Lord Abbott said in a cold tone, colder even than the air.

Anthony was struck by the difference in his friend, and, if her expression was anything to go by, so was Miss Denison. The smile faded from her pretty face, and she turned from Lord Abbott to extend shaking hands towards the growing fire.

Miss Myerson ran to the fire, also, relieving some of the tension. "Brrr, I did not realize it would be quite so cold."

"Nor did I, Miss Myerson. My apologies. Where is Miss Scott? I believe you ladies should remain here by the fire, and we will go about the business of finding the greenery as quickly as possible." Anthony waved to Mr. Scott to bring his daughter to the fire.

He then set the servants to work. Lord Abbott began to work with the other men, but Anthony noticed he moved in the opposite direction to his host. He frowned in puzzlement just as Thomas spoke to him.

"I say, Anthony, the snow is beautiful, but the cold is quite bitter."

"Yes, Thomas. We are hurrying with our gathering. Do you stay by the fire, or can you assist us?"

"Of course I shall assist you. That's what we came for."

"Yes. Do you know what is the matter with John?"

Thomas stopped in the act of pulling free a clump of mistletoe. "What do you mean?"

"He is avoiding me, and he was quite distant with Miss Denison." Anthony used the hatchet he had picked up from the pile of tools the servants had produced to cut several small branches from an evergreen tree.

"Must be the cold weather," Thomas assured him.

The weather was certainly cold enough to dampen someone's spirits, but Anthony did not believe it was the reason for his friend's behaviour. However, he had no other explanation.

"WHAT DO YOU THINK of this tree?" Sarah called out, only to discover she had no audience. She almost panicked, fearing she'd lost the children among the large trees, until she heard whispering. "Children?"

"Yes, Miss Barnes?" Melissa responded, peering from behind a tree several feet away.

"What are you doing? Have you found a tree?"

"Not yet."

"Where is Alistair?"

"He is here with me," Melissa assured her before disappearing behind the tree again.

Curiosity drove Sarah to follow Melissa. When she rounded the tree, she heard Alistair protesting, "No, I do not want to."

"But you must, Alistair. How else will we—" Melissa broke off as Alistair's eyes widened in fear.

Whirling round, the little girl stared at her governess. "Oh, Miss Barnes. Did you find a tree?"

"I found several," she replied dryly. "But it appears I am the only one looking. Have you found a tree?"

"No. But we will. Let's spread out and look again."

"I think it is too cold for you to continue. Let's return to the others."

Melissa readily agreed after giving her brother a significant stare that Sarah found interesting. Alistair, however, seemed reluctant.

"Alistair, aren't you cold?" Sarah was. Her cloak was inadequate for the strength of a winter storm and she was shaking.

"We must find a tree," the boy said stubbornly, not moving.

"I'm sure your father will have found one already, dear, and I am very cold." She watched with tenderness in her heart as her plea was immediately met.

He rushed to her side and offered his hand. "Of course, Miss Barnes. We shall go back at once."

Melissa skipped ahead of them, unaffected by the cold, and Sarah and Alistair followed. The sight of the large fire now burning near the carriages was heartening to Sarah, who had seriously begun to doubt her ability to walk much farther because of her shaking.

"Miss Barnes," Mr. Whitfield called as he caught sight of them. "I was becoming worried."

"Th-the children and I w-were searching for a t-tree," she muttered, not slowing in her approach to the fire.

"She is very cold, Father," she heard Alistair say, even as she reached out to the flame.

"Cedric, bring a robe from the coach," Mr. Whitfield called to one of the servants. Before Sarah realized what was happening, he was wrapping one of the fur robes about her.

"I should have realized your cloak was inadequate. Why did you not say anything?"

"W-we did not have such s-storms in Town often," she muttered. "I had no need of a h-heavier cloak."

"Come, Miss Barnes," Miss Denison said, "sit beside me." One of the servants had pulled a large log near the fire for her convenience.

She did so, already feeling a little better. The other two ladies were seated across from them, well protected from the storm.

"Th-the children?" she asked, looking up at her employer.

"They are fine. We shall be finished shortly. Are you feeling quite the thing?" Mr. Whitfield asked, reminding Sarah of the concern his son had shown only a few minutes before.

"Yes, of course."

After he left them to return to his work, Miss Denison smiled at Sarah. "He is such a considerate man."

"Yes," Sarah agreed, but her heart sank as she realized her plan to bring her employer and Miss Denison together was working.

CHAPTER SIX

By THE TIME they returned to the carriages, the snow was flying thick and fast, a snowstorm the like of which Sarah had never seen before.

The servants had refilled the foot warmers with coals from the bonfire, and Mr. Whitfield had assisted Sarah into his own carriage, tucking the robe round her most solicitously. She allowed herself the pleasure of riding with him and the children just this once. Beside, she was too cold to think about anything else.

"Th-the snow is lovely," she whispered, looking out at the magical flakes, distinctive until they blended with their brothers on the ever-deepening banks.

"Yes. Are you warm enough?"

"Yes, sir. Thank you for your kindness."

"I should have noticed your cloak before. In fact, I might have if you had ridden with us, as I'd planned." He stared at her, making Sarah nervous.

"Miss Denison—"

"She is not very pretty," Melissa said almost sullenly for one with her sunny personality.

Both adults turned to stare at the child across from them. Sarah said, "Do you mean Miss Denison? She is quite beautiful, Melissa."

"Not as beautiful as you," the child insisted, and nudged her brother with her elbow.

"Yes." Alistair seemed torn between remaining silent and supporting his sister.

"Thank you, children, but when you are better acquainted with Miss Denison, you will think her very beautiful." Sarah avoided looking at her employer. "She looks a great deal like your mother, if the portrait in the morning-room is anything to go by."

"I don't remember Mama," Melissa said with a distinct sniff.

Sarah's soft heart immediately opened to the child, as did her arms, and Melissa left her warm cocoon of fur robes to dive into Sarah's embrace.

Anthony didn't think Melissa was in too great distress, but a look at Alistair made him change his place in the carriage. Melissa might not remember her mother, but Alistair did. He'd been his sister's age when his mother had died. Now he looked forlorn.

"I guess we gentlemen must stick together, son, since the ladies are cuddling on the other seat. I think it will be warmer if I am here with you." He wrapped his arm around his son's shoulders and pulled him to his side.

Sarah beamed at him from across the coach, and he smiled ruefully. Her greatest approval of him came from his care of his children.

"When the storm has passed, perhaps tomorrow, shall we go sledding?" he asked, hoping to bring about a more cheerful atmosphere.

"Oh, yes!" Melissa agreed, brightening instantly.

"You mean go outside in the snow?"

He laughed at Sarah's incredulous look. "Yes, my dear, go outside in the snow. Have you never played in the snow?"

She shook her head. "I have only lived in cities all my life. The snow there is so dirty and...and it is cold."

"Ah. Well, we will have to find you something else to wear so that you can build your first snowman. I believe my mother's winter cloak is in the attics. I will look for it."

"Oh, no, I could not!"

"We will see," he said, though he was determined to care for Sarah as well as she cared for his children. To change the subject, he induced the silent Alistair to tell about the last snowman they'd built, before his mother's death.

The mood had lightened considerably by the time they arrived at the house. Anthony assisted Sarah and Melissa from the coach and then Alistair. After sending them into the warmth indoors, he hurried to the other carriages to ensure his guests' comfort.

Miss Scott, Miss Myerson and their fathers were in the second coach. "Hurry in at once," Anthony urged. "There will be warm drinks to take off the chill."

As the third carriage pulled to a halt, he swung open the door and discovered the same kind of gloom he'd dispelled in his own coach.

"Is all well?" he asked as he offered a hand to Miss Denison.

"Of course, Mr. Whitfield," she responded, but nary a smile crossed her lips. When she reached the ground, she gathered her cloak about her and rushed into the house. Her haste might have been due to the snowstorm, but Anthony thought otherwise, particularly when he saw Lord Abbott's face.

A scowl of immense proportions on his handsome features, he ignored Anthony's offer of assistance to descend. "I can manage," he growled.

"Is aught amiss, John?"

"Nothing," his friend threw over his shoulder as he charged through the flakes of snow.

Anthony waited for Mr. Denison to get out and enter the house and then turned back to Thomas, who was now exiting the carriage. "Did they have an argument?"

"Who?"

"John and Miss Denison. They were the only other occupants in your carriage besides Miss Denison's father, and I doubt that anyone would quarrel with him."

"I don't see how she and John could've argued. They only spoke a few words, and those as frozen as the countryside."

Anthony stood there puzzling over the situation, remembering John's dreamy expression the evening before when he had declared his love for Miss Denison. Clearly something had gone wrong.

"Must we stand here in the midst of a snowstorm worrying over John's love life?" Thomas demanded, shivering.

"No, of course not." Anthony hurried inside with his friend, anxious to see if matters had improved in the warmth of the house.

Clayton was waiting to remove their outer garments and steer them into the morning-room, where hot cider was being served.

"Be sure the servants receive a hot drink and plenty of time around the fire, Clayton. It was miserably cold out there."

"Yes, Mr. Whitfield."

He discovered no sign of a thaw in the morning-room, in spite of the huge fire roaring in the grate and the warm cups of cider being passed around.

"Thank you all for braving the outdoors in such a storm. I believe we have more than enough decorations for the house, do we not, Miss Barnes?"

"Yes, sir. It was most generous of your guests to assist us."

"I'm afraid," Miss Denison said with a lovely smile, "you gentlemen are the ones who suffered. We received such tender care that I scarce felt the cold. Thank you, Mr. Whitfield."

Of course such lovely sentiments must immediately be echoed and improved upon by Mrs. Myerson on her daughter's behalf, and Miss Scott, nudged by her mother, agreed.

"Where are the children?" Anthony asked as soon as everyone had settled by the fire.

Sarah answered at once. "I sent them to the nursery. Nanny Buckets had warm chocolate waiting for them. Perhaps I'd best check on them now that you are here to tend to your guests.'' Even as she spoke, Sarah was edging towards the door.

''I'm sure they are fine,'' he protested, but she slipped from the room, anyway.

''A most dedicated governess,'' Thomas said. ''You are quite fortunate in Miss Barnes,'' he informed his friend, an approving look on his face.

''So you have told me,'' Anthony growled, then realized he sounded remarkably as John had earlier.

SARAH DID NOT SEE any of the house party the rest of the afternoon. There was much to be done in preparation for the dinner party Mr. Whitfield was hosting for his neighbours and guests the next evening. Mrs. Clayton depended on Sarah to show her just how to go on.

Though she'd never spent time in Town, Sarah had been in Brighton for a Season, when she'd experienced the blow that had broken her heart. She put her exposure to the ton to good use now.

When she finally descended to dinner, the bitter cold of the afternoon was only a memory, but the results of their work could be seen throughout the house. Much of the greenery had been used to decorate the mantel in the parlour, tied together with silver and red bows, with candles interspersed through it.

Several of the maids had prepared the kissing bough, amidst much giggling, and Sarah had had it hung from the chandelier in the centre of the room. The big fir tree

Mr. Whitfield had chosen was standing in one corner, as yet unadorned. That task would have to wait until tomorrow.

When she entered the room, breathless because she was late, she found everyone else ahead of her. Mr. Whitfield stepped forward at once and extended a hand. She reluctantly put her own in his, and he led her to the others.

"My dear, you have done a marvellous job with the decorations. My congratulations."

To her surprise, everyone applauded.

"But...but it is not finished yet," she murmured, embarrassed by the attention.

"Ah, then we have more to look forward to. Splendid."

He tried to lead her to the centre of the room, but Sarah pulled him to a halt. When he urged her forward, she refused and leaned over to whisper in his ear. "Sir, the kissing bough is just ahead. If you will excuse me?"

She slipped from his grasp and moved away to greet Mrs. Scott. A quick glance over her shoulder showed her employer staring after her.

Surely the man had not intended to lead her under the kissing bough? Her cheeks flaming, she turned her back on him. She would not be sport for a man about to be married!

"You did not give me the opportunity to explain a change in our arrangements," Mr. Whitfield murmured in her ear.

She jumped in surprise, not having realized he'd followed her, and turned to look at him. A knowing twinkle in his eye told her he had read her thoughts about the kissing bough. She blushed in irritation. "What is it, sir?" She dared him by her very tones to mention the ridiculous decoration. He disconcerted her by discussing another subject completely.

"I have decided you are right. It is not fair to expect you to perform the duties of hostess at dinner each evening as well as all your other responsibilities. So I have asked Mrs. Myerson to sit in the hostess's chair this evening and Mrs. Scott tomorrow evening."

That explained the gracious smile Mrs. Myerson had given her when she entered, Sarah thought with unaccustomed cynicism. She also wondered what she had done to disappoint Mr. Whitfield. But she could not ask.

"Of course, sir. Thank you for your thoughtfulness." She did not meet his gaze. Fortunately, Clayton entered at that moment to announce dinner.

Thomas Crutcher appeared at Sarah's elbow and extended his arm. "May I escort you to dinner, Miss Barnes?"

"No, I—" Mr. Whitfield began.

Sarah cut him off before he could finish his thought. "Thank you, Mr. Crutcher. That is most generous in you."

Her employer was left to extend his arm to Mrs. Scott. When Mr. Crutcher led her into the dining-hall behind Lord Abbott and Mrs. Myerson, her escort headed to the foot of the table.

"Oh, no, Mr. Crutcher," Sarah whispered just as Lord Abbott pulled out the chair for Mrs. Myerson. "Mr. Whitfield has asked Mrs. Myerson to be hostess this evening."

"But where are you to—"

"Everyone will note the new seating arrangement," Mr. Whitfield called out. "We have used place cards this evening to add some variety to our meal."

Lord Abbott still remained in the place of honour, as was his due as the only titled gentleman present, but the other diners had been rearranged. Mr. Crutcher discovered his companion would be Mrs. Myerson.

With a sigh, he escorted Sarah round the table until they reached the last seat, next to her host and across from Lord Abbott.

"Huh!" Thomas grunted, frowning at his friend. "Why must I keep the same place?"

Anthony grinned at his friend's displeasure. "Because you have such exquisite manners, you will charm Mrs. Myerson."

Thomas only shot him a black glance and returned down the table to greet his dinner partner. Sarah stood awkwardly by her chair. "Sir, shouldn't Miss Denison—"

He held her chair and gestured for her to be seated, ignoring her attempted question.

Once everyone was settled, Anthony sat down and motioned to Clayton for the meal to begin. Bowls of hot soup were placed in front of everyone.

"Now you can switch your soup with mine if you have any fears of Mrs. Myerson," he teased, leaning close to Sarah.

"Please, sir, I was only joking," she hastily assured him in a whisper, and picked up her spoon.

With Sarah concentrating on her soup, Anthony turned to the friend who'd avoided him all afternoon and said in a low voice, "I apologize for removing Miss Denison, but it would have been too obvious to keep her beside you, John."

His friend glared at him before turning to do the pretty with Miss Scott, his new dinner companion.

Anthony stared at him in surprise, then addressed his attention to his soup. It appeared he would have no conversation with his neighbours, at least for a while.

"The children took no harm from the cold?" he finally asked Sarah after the fish had been served. The children were always a safe topic.

"No, I think not, but we did not accomplish much in the schoolroom. They were too eager to discuss the snowstorm and sledding on the morrow."

"Do not be concerned about studies this week. After all, we have another purpose to pursue, do we not?" When she attacked her fish with total concentration, Anthony frowned. What had he said wrong this time?

"I believe I shall have to depart on the morrow," John said suddenly, catching his attention.

"What?" Anthony asked, startled. "But you promised to stay all week. Why would you leave now?"

"I have pressing business."

"Where? It cannot be in Town, because you have received no communication from there since we departed, and you planned to remain here all week." Anthony laid down his fork and knife as he remembered. "In fact, you said you did not plan to return to Town until early spring."

"Well, I have changed my mind," John said dourly, refusing to look at his friend.

"Well, unchange it. You gave your word."

"You are asking too much, sir!" John replied, his voice rising.

"Gentlemen!" Sarah called fiercely. When she gained their attention, she added in a low voice, "If you must argue, could you not do so after dinner, when the ladies have withdrawn? The others are staring."

Both men's faces flushed at their breach of good conduct. "My apologies," Anthony said to everyone. "Lord Abbott and I were . . . were discussing my acquiring the pup of one of his prime hunting dogs. He is quite attached to them."

The smile on John's lips reassured Anthony. He did not know what he had done to offend his friend, but he would discover the cause before the night ended.

"I love doggieth," Miss Scott said softly, her lisp in evidence.

"Do you?" Lord Abbott replied politely, but his lips quivered.

Anthony turned to Sarah and was surprised to discover a guilty look on her face.

"What do you know about John's sudden decision?" he demanded, sure that she'd overheard their words.

"About the hunting dog?" she asked politely, but he noticed she did not look at him.

"Sarah," he said quietly, smiling when her head snapped up. "No, I know I should call you Miss Barnes, but I feel we are friends." He waited for her to acknowledge his words, but she only looked away. "Do you know why John has decided to leave?"

"He . . . he has said nothing to me of leaving."

She toyed with her fish, avoiding his gaze. He sensed a loneliness that he wanted to dispel, and had a sudden urge to draw her into his arms, to cuddle her against him as he might Melissa. Until he thought about it. And then it wasn't like hugging Melissa at all.

He took a sip of wine, hoping to rid his mind of the image of Sarah in his arms, her warm curves pressed against his hardness, her blue eyes wide with desire—

The wine was not helping at all.

He signalled for the next course to be served. The sooner he could put some distance between the fetching young lady beside him and himself, the better his self-control would be.

"We shall talk after the ladies have withdrawn," he murmured to John as he saw Miss Scott turn to Mr. Myerson, seated on her right.

"There is nothing to talk about," John said hastily. Anthony wasn't going to let him escape that easily.

The meal seemed interminable, with his friend angry with him for some unknown reason and Sarah too tempting for him to be comfortable. When Mrs. Myerson made a signal for the women to withdraw, Anthony felt like rising and giving a cheer.

As soon as the door closed behind the ladies, he stood and looked at Thomas. "Would you mind playing host to the other gentlemen? John and I have something we must discuss in private."

"Of course, Tony," Thomas responded, but his eyes conveyed his intent for revenge. He'd already suffered through Mrs. Myerson as a dinner companion. Now his two friends were excluding him.

"Thank you, Thomas. Gentlemen, please excuse us," Anthony said apologetically, even as he grasped an unwilling John's arm.

When they reached the hallway, John pulled free. "Really, Tony, I suppose I may choose to leave when I wish. I am no prisoner, am I?"

"Of course you are not a prisoner," Anthony assured his friend. "I only wish to discover what I have done to anger you. We are friends, John. I would not want to lose that friendship."

Lord Abbott looked away, pain on his face. "No. Nor would I. Just . . . just give me some time, Tony. I will recover, and I will wish you well."

"Wish me well?" Anthony studied his friend's face. "Why would you do so?"

"You are to be married, are you not? That is what you told me. It is customary to . . . to wish one's friend well at such a time." Still John would not look at him.

"I refuse to have this discussion in the hall for all to hear. Come to the library with me," Anthony insisted, but he did not attempt to force his friend to accompany him. He was relieved when he heard John's footsteps following his own.

Once the door had been closed behind them, Anthony invited his friend to sit down and he poured them both a glass of port. John took it and stared down into the depths of the glass.

"John, I do not understand the difficulty. Are you upset that I am considering remarriage? Last night you were in favour of it. You, also, spoke of marrying."

His friend's head came up and he glared at Anthony. "That was cruel, Tony. I had not thought it of you."

"But what have I done? I am not trying to displease you. I would never do that!"

"You are marrying Claire. That wounds me beyond belief," John told him, closing his eyes in agony.

Anthony stared at him, stunned. Finally, he said, "But who is Claire? I cannot marry her if I do not know who she is."

CHAPTER SEVEN

"MISS DENISON!" John exclaimed, staring at Anthony in horror.

Anthony returned his look, wondering if John had lost his mind. Then he said, "Do you mean Miss Denison is Claire?"

"Yes, of course she is! You must know that if you are to marry her."

"I am not marrying Miss Denison. You said you were."

"*You* have first claim upon her. But I wish you had been honest with me."

Anthony leapt from his chair, his glass tightly gripped in his hand. "I have not been dishonest! I am not marrying Miss Denison. I wished you well! Do you not remember?"

John stood and angrily returned, "Of course I remember! But I thought you had changed your mind!"

The two men glared at each other until silence and consideration cooled their ire. Finally Anthony asked, "Why would you think I changed my mind? What did I do to make you think that?"

"You took her up in your carriage today," John pointed out, anger rising again.

"That was not my doing. I was surprised to find her there."

"You mean she *chose* to ride with you?" John's anger dissolved into despair.

"No, I do not think so," Anthony said slowly, dismay overwhelming him. "I believe Miss Barnes arranged everything thinking to assist me."

"Why do you say so?"

Anthony shook his head, unwilling to explain his deductions or to allow his friend to see how devastating they were. "It does not matter. But rest assured I have not set my sights on Miss Denison. I already look upon her as the wife of my best friend and near neighbour."

John beamed at him. "I only hope Claire will cooperate with your vision."

They returned to the hall just as the other men emerged from the dining-room.

"Shall we join the ladies?" Anthony asked, smiling at Thomas.

With mutual agreement, they all turned to the drawing room, where the ladies were waiting. Thomas, however, clutched Anthony's shoulder before they entered.

"I shall take my vengeance upon you, friend," Thomas whispered, "for abandoning me twice in one evening."

"Twice? I remember only once, and I do appreciate it, Thomas."

"Twice," Thomas reiterated firmly. "First with Mrs. Myerson for a dinner partner while you enjoyed Miss Barnes. 'Twas unfair."

"You are right. But I could not continue to expose Miss Barnes to Mrs. Myerson's ire."

"Very well. But I shall sit with Miss Barnes now. *You* may entertain that woman!"

Anthony shrugged. If his suppositions were correct, he would have no luck conversing with Miss Barnes this evening, anyway. She appeared to favour Miss Denison for his bride.

As they entered the drawing-room, he realized that neither of them was in luck. Miss Barnes had already withdrawn, pleading additional chores to perform for the next day.

Anthony passed a deadly dull evening.

SARAH ROSE the next morning with much still to do. She had found it difficult to concentrate on her chores the evening before while she worried about her employer and his friend.

Mr. Whitfield would be unhappy if Lord Abbott left the party early, but remaining must be difficult for Lord Abbott if he, too, wanted to marry Miss Denison. And lucky Miss Denison, to have two such eligible gentlemen pursuing her.

Sarah immediately shut away such traitorous thoughts. She was content with her lot in life. She truly was. But a shiver of longing could not be suppressed when she thought of Mr. Whitfield.

"Miss Barnes! Are we going to decorate the tree this morning?" Melissa asked as she ran into the schoolroom.

"We must make the bows first. I was only able to make a few for the mantel yesterday. I thought we would ask the ladies to assist us."

Alistair, who followed his sister into the room, asked, "Must we accompany you?"

Sarah looked at his unhappy face and reached out to touch his forehead. "Darling, are you feeling all right? You do not have a fever, do you?"

"No, Miss Barnes. But I had rather read than sit with the ladies making bows." The disgust in his voice reassured Sarah. After all, he was a boy.

"Of course, Alistair. You may remain here, if you like, and read. Nanny Buckets will be in the next room with Justin if you need anything." She turned to Melissa. "Will you stay with Alistair?"

"Oh, no. I want to make bows," Melissa said, a bright smile on her face.

"Very well. Alistair, why do you not come down to the morning-room with us for a little while? The other ladies will not be there yet, and we shall have tea and perhaps some gingerbread. I believed I smelled it when I was downstairs, earlier."

Gingerbread was Alistair's favourite treat. The indecision on his face almost brought a smile to Sarah's face.

"And I may return to the schoolroom after tea?" he asked carefully.

"Yes, dear."

With that assurance, he accompanied Sarah and Melissa to the morning-room. Sarah gave the children the task of measuring the ribbon and cutting it into pieces for the bows. She took on the prickly chore of making a holly wreath.

The three of them worked contentedly at their tasks. The fragrant scent of gingerbread and evergreens made the crackling of the fire and the silent scattering of snowflakes on the windowpane seem cosy and comforting.

Anthony found them there and stood in the doorway, longing to be a part of the charming scene. When Melissa spied him watching them, she welcomed him happily. Alistair, too, had a smile for his father. Sarah quickly returned her gaze to her task.

"May I join you?" he asked, unsure of his welcome after his discoveries on the previous evening.

"Of course, Mr. Whitfield. If you ring for Clayton, he will bring a new pot of tea and more gingerbread."

"I should hate to put him to such trouble only for myself. Will anyone eat more gingerbread with me?"

Though his father looked first at Miss Barnes, Alistair nodded eagerly. Anthony laughed and pulled the bell-rope.

After their tray had been replenished, he took a seat near Sarah and watched her efforts.

"Does it not hurt when it sticks you?" he asked.

"Ouch!" She glared at him as if the nick from the holly was his fault. "Yes, sir." She sucked on the wound.

He drew a deep breath, fighting the desire that rose in him. She looked up at him, then quickly turned away.

"Miss Barnes," Melissa said, interrupting the silent conversation. "I have been thinking. Your Christmas Angel would look very nice atop the tree. Could we borrow it?"

Sarah considered Melissa's words. "I suppose it would not hurt if your father does not object."

"Of course I do not," Anthony replied. He liked the idea, something of Sarah gracing their tree, as if she were part of the family.

"Let's put it on the tree now, before the others come down," Melissa insisted, jumping up and down in her excitement. "Alistair and I will fetch it."

"Very well. We shall need a ladder," Sarah added, frowning as she tried to consider all that would be necessary.

"I'll have one of the footmen bring one," Anthony said, following his children from the room.

When they all came together in the parlour where the tall evergreen stood in one corner, Melissa carried the Christmas Angel gently in her arms, a beatific smile on her little face.

"Isn't she beautiful? Just like Miss Barnes."

Sarah's cheeks flamed and she said nothing. Anthony could not resist responding. "They are both angels."

Melissa beamed, and even Alistair smiled at his father before the pair exchanged a significant look. Anthony wondered what his children were up to.

"Will you place the angel on the tree, sir?" Sarah asked hurriedly, ignoring his words.

"I believe you should have that privilege, Sarah. After all, she is your angel." He stepped back from the ladder a footman had placed next to the tree.

She took the doll from Melissa and moved to the ladder. Lifting her skirts, she climbed the steps. Anthony stood near the ladder, concerned with her safety.

"Be careful, Sarah."

"Yes, sir." She stretched over and placed the doll upright among the branches at the top of the tree. "Does it suit?"

"It is wonderful!" Melissa shouted.

"She is perfect there, Miss Barnes," chimed in Alistair.

Sarah turned round to smile down at her audience and lost her balance.

Fortunately, Anthony had not taken his eyes off her. When she began to fall, he moved a few steps and received her into his arms as if he'd planned it.

"Ooooh!" Sarah cried, her eyes wide with fright. Her arms encircled the squire's neck, clinging to him for safety.

Anthony's arms tightened, pressing her slim form against his chest. Their gazes met and the heat that rose in him was greater than that of by the fire.

"Miss Barnes, are you all right?" Alistair demanded, rushing to his father's side.

Melissa reached up to pluck at her governess's skirts. "You did not hurt yourself, did you? Papa did very well catching you, didn't he?"

"Y-yes, very well," Sarah said, turning her gaze away from the man holding her.

There was a moment of silence before Alistair said, "You can stand, can't you?"

Immediately Sarah struggled in Anthony's arms, and he reluctantly allowed her to slide down his body and step away. He had not wanted to release her. In fact, had the children not been present, he would have had the kiss he'd been thinking about for what seemed an eternity.

"I should not have allowed you to climb the ladder, Sarah. My apologies." In truth, he would not have traded for any price the past few moments of holding her in his arms.

He recognized now what he should have known days before. He had no interest in the other ladies because he had been bewitched by the governess. Sarah Barnes, her blazing beauty hidden in deplorable gray gowns, her warmth wrapped around his children, had caught his heart.

He had not believed anyone could supplant Larissa in his life, but his dead wife was becoming a fond memory, while Sarah, sweet Sarah, was demanding his love by her very presence. He wanted to hold her again.

BY THE TIME Sarah and Melissa returned to the morning-room, Sarah's heart had slowed its frantic beat. But she could still feel the imprint of Mr. Whitfield's arms around her.

"Miss Barnes?"

"What? Oh, yes, Melissa?"

"Why is Papa calling you Sarah?"

Sarah sought frantically for a reasonable answer. "Because...because I am dining with the others in the evenings."

"Oh."

Fortunately—since Sarah didn't think her inane answer would satisfy Melissa for long—Miss Denison entered the room.

"Good morning. Clayton suggested I join you here. Oh, are you doing more decorating?"

Sarah smiled at the beautiful young woman, envious of the elegant sprig muslin gown that swirled about her. She determined to be extra pleasant to make up for her envy.

"Yes, we are tying bows for the tree. Would you care to assist us?"

"I should love to," Miss Denison said with a smile, and settled down beside Melissa. "Are you helping Miss Barnes?"

"Yes," Melissa replied, but she didn't smile.

Mrs. Scott and her daughter entered, followed soon by Mrs. and Miss Myerson. Sarah organized more tea and gingerbread and encouraged the ladies to tie bows, then sat a little apart, withdrawing from their chatter. After all, she was not one of them. It was time to remember her place.

When she'd first offered to assist Mr. Whitfield, she had done so because she wanted the children to be happy, to have a mother. And she had been taught to assist where she was needed.

She had not recognized the danger. But it was very real. Dining with Mr. Whitfield's guests had tempted her to forget her lowly station and her uninspired future. Having the running of a large house under her order had given her an exalted but illusory sense of her position. Worst of all, being in Mr. Whitfield's company had caused her to lose her heart.

She already loved his children.

Now she loved him, yet she must help him win his bride.

And then she would have to go away.

"Are you all right, Miss Barnes?" Miss Denison asked, leaning towards her.

Sarah's head snapped up at the question and she swallowed the tears that threatened to overwhelm her. "Yes, of course. Is there something you need?"

"No, not at all. I just thought you looked sad."

Sarah only smiled and shrugged. At least Mr. Whitfield's choice was a kind young woman.

The gathering of ladies was invaded at that moment by two gentlemen. Mr. Crutcher and Lord Abbott strolled in.

"We have discovered where the ladies were hiding, Thomas," Lord Abbott said with a lazy grin, but Sarah noticed his gaze fixed immediately on Miss Denison.

"May we join you?" Thomas Crutcher asked, looking to Sarah for approval.

After her stern lecture to herself, she looked at the two older ladies for their approval.

Mrs. Myerson smiled and patted the sofa beside her. "Of course, Mr. Crutcher. I have been looking forward to conversing with you again."

Even in her sad state, Sarah felt the bubble of laughter rise up in her at Mr. Crutcher's quickly hidden dismay. Like a true gentleman, he assumed the place next to the lady and joined her in conversation.

Miss Denison kept her gaze lowered. When Lord Abbott headed towards her, Sarah intercepted him.

"My lord, have you seen Mr. Whitfield? I wondered if he would join us."

Lord Abbott paused only to say, "I haven't seen him," before stepping around her and joining Miss Denison.

Sarah sat back down and watched the two chat. Miss Denison appeared withdrawn at first, but Lord Abbott talked earnestly and long and soon she was smiling up at him.

"Miss Denison, would you help me collect the wonderful bows that everyone has made?" Sarah asked. If she couldn't keep Lord Abbott from Miss Denison, perhaps Sarah could remove Miss Denison from his clutches.

Lord Abbott rose with his companion and reached out to take the basket Sarah offered. "I shall play your knight, Miss Denison, and carry this heavy load for you."

Sarah stood there, watching the pair of them gather the ribbons in the basket, Lord Abbott teasing and smiling at Miss Denison as she blushed in return. This was not what Sarah had planned.

"Shall we plathe the bowth on the tree now, Mith Barneth?" Miss Scott asked.

"Yes, of course. Melissa, will you go and ask Alistair to join us? I am sure he wants to assist in decorating the tree." She turned to Lord Abbott for one last try at separating him from Miss Denison. "We also need Mr. Whitfield. Did you say you had seen him this morning, my lord?"

"I saw him," Mr. Crutcher said before his friend could answer. "Shall I go search for him, Miss Barnes? I shall be glad to do so."

Before Sarah could stop him, Mr. Crutcher was out the door, clearly eager to escape Mrs. Myerson.

"I have never decorated a tree before," Miss Myerson commented, giggling.

"We shall all enjoy a new experience," Lord Abbott said, smiling into Miss Denison's eyes.

Not if she could prevent it, Sarah promised herself. She didn't want the children disappointed, and they would be if Lord Abbott took Miss Denison away from their father.

Sarah led the way into the parlour, all the time searching for something to part the couple. Finally she asked Lord Abbott to ring for Clayton. As soon as he stepped away from Miss Denison's side, which he did with obvious reluctance, Sarah enlisted her help in demonstrating how to tie on the bows.

Relief filled her when Mr. Whitfield, along with Mr. Crutcher and Alistair, entered the room. Mr. Whitfield came at once to her side.

"Sir, could you perhaps hold the basket for Miss Denison? I must speak to Clayton about arrangements for this evening."

"Can it not wait until later? I thought we were all to decorate the tree together." He stared at her with a warmth in his eyes that reminded her of the time she had found herself in his arms.

She quickly moved away. "It will not take long. Assist Miss Denison, please." What was wrong with the man? She was providing him with an opportunity to court the woman of his choice, and he showed no interest.

Righteous anger welled within her at his lack of cooperation, yet underneath that emotion lurked envy, loneliness and heartsickness. She had to remember Christmas, and the happiness of the children she loved, she reminded herself, before the darker emotions took over.

Rather than talk to Clayton, Sarah slipped into the dining-room to note the arrangements for luncheon. Again, Mr. Whitfield had instructed the use of place cards. Sarah retrieved the one with her name, once more at her employer's left hand, and put it in Miss Scott's place. She then set Miss Scott's card at the place next to Lord Abbott's. She moved Miss Denison, who had for some reason been placed next to the one man her employer should hope to keep distant, to be next to Mr. Whitfield.

When she returned to the parlour, Lord Abbott was once more assisting Miss Denison, and Sarah almost stamped her foot in irritation. How did Mr. Whitfield expect to persuade the young woman to marry him when he did nothing to attach her? And how could Miss Denison prefer Lord Abbott to Mr. Whitfield?

Both gentlemen were handsome, of course, and Lord Abbott did have a title, but Mr. Whitfield was kind, loving to his children, caring... Sarah clamped down on her thoughts.

"Sarah! You have done a marvellous job. Come look at our efforts," Mr. Whitfield called.

Indeed, the tree was magnificent, its lush green branches now highlighted with red and silver bows. She smiled at the children, who stood with their father. "Do you like it?"

Alistair crossed to her side and took her hand. "It's beautiful, the most beautiful one we've ever had, especially 'cause of the Christmas Angel."

Sarah's doll, its white silk gown topping the tree, smiled down at them. "She does look like an angel, doesn't she, dear?"

Melissa joined them, catching Sarah's other hand. Sarah's gaze met Mr. Whitfield's, and she was surprised by the loneliness and desire she thought she read there. She urged the children back to their father's side and thanked the ladies for their efforts.

"Luncheon is almost ready. I am sure you are all hungry after your hard work."

"And you'd best eat hearty at luncheon, because this afternoon we're going sledding," Mr. Whitfield added, catching her by surprise. "I promised the children we'd try out the hill behind the house. Everyone is welcome to join us."

Her heart leapt at the thought of sliding down the hill on a sled. She'd never been sledding in her life. Even more enticing was the unbidden thought of doing so in Mr. Whitfield's arms. That image brought the blood rushing to her cheeks and caused her to resolve to remain indoors. She could not give in to such foolish desires.

CHAPTER EIGHT

ANTHONY WATCHED Sarah as he announced their afternoon plans. He enjoyed the flush that filled her cheeks, making him want to warm his hands against her face. But the stark resolve that filled her eyes immediately afterwards warned him his intent would not be easily achieved. With a sigh of frustration, he resolved to be patient.

When all were gathered round the table for luncheon a few minutes later, however, his resolve faltered. Finding Miss Denison beside him, rather than Sarah, he glowered at the young woman farther down the table who, he felt sure, had rearranged the seating.

"I thought you wished me well?" John muttered on his right.

"You know I do."

"Then why is Claire not beside me?"

"For the same reason she rode in my carriage yesterday," Anthony admitted with a sigh. "My Christmas Angel does not understand."

"Christmas Angel? You are referring to the one on the tree?" John asked, his gaze fixed on Miss Denison.

Anthony ignored his distracted friend's question. He was watching Sarah converse with Mr. Myerson, her warmth making that gentleman more open and relaxed than usual. She *was* an angel, always helping others. His staff loved her, his children adored her, and he . . . he was swiftly becoming obsessed with her.

"Do not worry," he finally said to John. "We shall have the arranging of partners for the sledding. That is more desirable than dining next to someone."

Those words caught John's attention. "Ah, yes," he agreed, almost rubbing his hands together in anticipation. "Sledding together. Miss Denison and I shall be the first ones down."

"It is my hill. I think I should be the one to go down first. Just to see if it is safe, of course. And Miss Barnes must ensure its safety for the children," Anthony said, his gaze never leaving the governess.

"Why do you not tell Miss Barnes that you have no interest in Miss Denison?" John asked abruptly. "Then she would not attempt to place you next to Claire."

Before Anthony could answer, Miss Scott, on Lord Abbott's right, claimed John's attention. Anthony turned to Miss Denison to make conversation, but his mind churned with the implications of his friend's question.

He *had* intended to talk to Sarah, to explain John's interest in Miss Denison. But he realized that when he did so, Sarah would know he had no intention of wedding any of the three ladies he'd invited as his guests.

After all, he had already eliminated Miss Myerson, and the children did not care for Miss Scott. Therefore, the pretence that he was to select a bride could not be continued. And he feared Sarah would then retreat to the schoolroom, making it impossible to court her as he wanted.

Therefore, he had decided to keep everything secret until John officially declared for Miss Denison. He would just have to counteract Sarah's well-intentioned efforts to place him and Miss Denison together.

What concerned him most was Sarah's determination on the match. Did that mean she had no interest in him? When he had held her in his arms, he would have sworn she felt something, too. Her first flush of enthusiasm for the sledding had been encouraging, also.

He gave a firm nod, determined to keep his spirits high. Miss Denison stared at him in surprise. "You agree?"

"I beg your pardon? I did not—that is, I was distracted." He reluctantly drew his eyes from Sarah to look at his dinner companion.

Miss Denison's gaze travelled down the table and back, and she smiled at her host. "Ah. I had not realized. I thought—" She broke off in confusion. "That is, when you invited us all—" Again she stopped.

"That was my intent," Anthony hurriedly agreed, embarrassed, as well. "You see, my children...I felt it was time to remarry."

Miss Denison nodded. "I understand. But I am much relieved. You see, my interests are—that is . . . I am glad." Her cheeks were bright red, and after a lightning-quick glance across the table at Lord Abbott, she concentrated on her plate.

Anthony nodded in satisfaction. He and Miss Denison were in complete understanding. Why couldn't he reach the same state with the frustrating young lady now entertaining Mr. Myerson?

SARAH WATCHED Mr. Whitfield and Miss Denison conversing and felt the tiny sprig of hope that hid in her heart die away as Miss Denison responded with bright red cheeks. Clearly Mr. Whitfield was charming the woman.

That is what you wanted, is it not? she demanded of her contrary heart. *You complained when he did not take advantage of the opportunity while decorating the tree.* It had to be what she wanted, for the children, her beloved children. They wanted a mother, and Miss Denison was the best candidate of the three.

She tried to turn her attention back to Mr. Myerson, who, away from his wife, was a thoughtful and charming companion. But he could not hold a candle to Mr. Whitfield, she mournfully admitted. And after the Christmas holidays, Sarah knew she must pack her things and leave behind those she loved. The children. The staff. And most of all, Mr. Whitfield.

The meal ended and Mr. Whitfield warned those who wanted to go sledding to dress warmly and meet in the front hall in half an hour. She tried to slip up the stairs, but he caught her by the arm as she reached the first step.

"I found my mother's old cloak in the attic earlier," he said, a warm smile on his face. "It has been left in your room. Be sure to wear it. There are some boots she used, also. I hope they will fit you."

"I do not intend to accompany the children, sir. I did not think it would be necessary, and there is much to be done for this evening." She avoided his bright gaze.

"This evening matters not, Sarah. You shall go sledding with the rest of us."

Such an outrageous statement brought her eyes to his. "Sir, how can you say such a thing? This evening is your first entertainment in the neighbourhood in several years, and I am sure you will want everything in order."

"My neighbours know I am out of practice as a host. Whatever hospitality I offer will be accepted." He smiled at her. "You and I are to be first down the hill." He quickly added, "Just to test the safety for my children, of course. It is your duty."

Her duty. Sarah stared into his warm grey eyes and could not resist his command. She would give herself this one afternoon as a gift. Sledding for the first time. Sledding with Mr. Whitfield and his children. A Christmas gift, a memory worth treasuring.

"Very well, sir, if it is my duty." She could not hold back a smile that showed her excitement. "I will prepare the children."

As she flew up the stairs, the caution she tried to remember disappeared. Yes, she would have one afternoon of pleasure to hold next to her heart in the long, lonely years ahead.

ANTHONY had had the servants build a fire on the hilltop where the sledders might warm themselves. By the time he led his troop of energetic guests along with his children and Sarah to the highest part of the hill, the fire was burning brightly, a red flame in a white-and-green world.

The snow had stopped midway through the morning and it glistened in the reappearing sunlight. Their breath formed clouds of white in front of them, and laughter rang in the clear air.

"I am so excited. We did not sled last year, and before, Papa said I was too young," Melissa explained, hopping along as she held Sarah's hand.

"You must be very careful and do exactly as your father says," Sarah cautioned. She tried to caution herself as well, but she was as excited as Melissa.

Alistair, who'd been walking with his father, suddenly turned and came running back to Sarah. "Miss Barnes, Father said you and he must take the first run to see if it is safe for us. Do hurry. I can hardly wait to slide down!"

Sarah smiled down at his face, lit up with expectation. It filled her heart with joy to see the normally solemn child smiling at her so merrily. It almost made her forget the ride in store for her. Almost.

"Come, Sarah," Mr. Whitfield called. "It's time to try your courage."

Sarah responded to his smile, knowing her courage would be tested, but not by the hill. Her heart was much more in danger than her limbs.

Looking at the sled she was to ride, however, made her re-evaluate the danger. It did not appear large enough for one person, much less two. "We are to ride that?"

"Never fear, I shall see you safely to the bottom," Mr. Whitfield assured her, a wicked grin on his handsome face.

She swallowed and then nodded. Very well. She would trust him. He instructed her to sit on the front of the sled. She did so, tucking the cloak and her long skirts about her boots, her knees folded up against her.

Then Mr. Whitfield joined her, his legs coming around her, his arms settling around her waist. Even in the cold, she felt a warmth stealing up inside her at his nearness. "Is . . . is this customary?" she asked faintly.

"Absolutely necessary," he whispered in one ear and pulled her even more tightly against him. "You must relax, Sarah. Allow me to protect you."

She took a deep breath and tried to follow his instructions. After all, it was her duty. A hysterical bubble of laughter rose in her at such a ridiculous thought. Before she could admit that nothing could have torn her from his arms at this point, he gave a shout to the others and they were off.

His cheek resting against hers, his arms holding her tightly, Sarah didn't even notice as the trees whizzed past her at a frightening speed. She had never travelled at such a breathtaking pace. She clutched Mr. Whitfield's arms, wondering if she would survive her first sledding experience.

When they slowed down, she realized they had reached the bottom of the hill in only seconds. Though there was a wide, open area at the bottom, their sled ran among several trees.

It came to rest with the crunchy protest of new snow, and Sarah finally breathed normally. "Oh, my, I have never—that was most exhilarating. Thank you, Mr. Whitfield, for—" She never finished her thought, because her employer had turned and covered her lips with his.

Her resolve had given way to abandon with the thrill of sledding, and Sarah had no chance to resist his touch. It would have taken a much sterner woman not to respond to his warm lips, his overpowering presence. She met him, kiss for kiss, until he lifted his face.

"As much as I should like to continue, dear Sarah, I must signal our safety or the entire group will head down the hill to see about us," he said huskily, his eyes caressing her almost as intimately as his lips had done.

Recalled to her circumstances, Sarah was filled with dismay, the blood rushing from her cheeks, leaving her cold and alone. She turned away from him as he rose from the sled and moved back to the open to wave to the others.

She scrambled to her feet and grabbed the rope on the front of the sled. Taking a more direct route to the top of the hill, she hoped to put some distance between herself and Mr. Whitfield.

He shouted when he saw her and she could hear his boots crunching into the deep snow, but she kept her head down and continued on her way. Concentrating on the bright sunshine, the shimmering whiteness of the snow, the cold air, anything but what had happened among the trees, she climbed higher.

"Sarah! Wait!"

Still she ignored him. Only when his arm snaked around her waist, forcing her to halt, did she stop. "Please, Mr. Whitfield, the children are waiting." She kept her chin tucked into the muffler she'd wrapped around her, hoping to avoid his gaze.

"We shall join them at once, of course, Sarah, but I shall pull the sled. I shall even give you a ride if you grow tired." She heard the teasing in his voice, but she refused to look at him. Surrendering the rope to his hands, she trudged on ahead.

"Sarah, are you angry with me? I could not resist congratulating you on your first sled ride."

Congratulating her! Perhaps she wasn't as knowledgeable about the ton as she'd thought. Could it be that such behaviour was sanctioned by the gentry? No, she did not think so. Perhaps young bucks behaved in such a way, but not with the women they intended to marry. Only with servants, governesses, shop-girls or worse.

"You would not have behaved so with Miss Denison," she muttered, hoping to hold back the tears that thickened her voice.

"Of course not. I do not—"

A shout from the top interrupted him, and they both looked up to see Lord Abbott and Miss Denison slide past them, wrapped together as they themselves had been only a few minutes before.

Sarah surged ahead and joined the others round the fire.

"Was it wonderful?" Alistair demanded, his eager eyes trained on her.

"Yes, it was wonderful, dear, but ever so fast. I think you should go down before Melissa. Why don't you ask your father to take you?"

Alistair didn't hesitate to do her bidding, running to his father's side at once to relate his governess's suggestion. Melissa, on the other hand, protested loudly to Sarah about having to wait even longer for her treat.

Sarah stood there, not really listening to Melissa, watching as Mr. Whitfield placed his son at the front of the sled before joining him. Just as they received a push from the servants, he turned and his eyes met Sarah's.

An unbidden wish to be in Alistair's place, to slide down the hill in her employer's arms, to receive his "congratulations" at the bottom of the hill, filled her with frightening strength.

Ah, yes, she must definitely leave as soon as Christmas was ended. And she must avoid the dangerously handsome man who filled her thoughts. But for one shimmering moment, she'd been wrapped in his arms, his lips caressing hers, just as they had in her dreams.

ANTHONY TOOK first Alistair and then Melissa down the hill and repeated his efforts as the children clamoured for more. He only caught glimpses of Sarah as she saw to his guests' comfort.

Memory of their ride together filled him with desire to repeat it, but Sarah clearly wanted no part of him. That had not been the case when his lips had met hers. He'd been surprised, then thrilled, when she'd warmed to his touch, snuggling closer rather than pulling away.

Her words afterwards bothered him, however. At first he thought she was finally realizing he did not care for Miss Denison. Then, as he climbed the hill with the excited Alistair beside him, he realized she thought he had showed her disrespect, not admiration.

His lips curved in a tender smile. She did not understand, but she would. He would talk to her this evening, as soon as their guests retired. He would ask her to stay behind as the other women went upstairs, and then he would draw her to the kissing bough.

The thought of taking her lips once more, of holding her in his arms, without the hindrance of their winter clothing, sent a surge of desire through him. Ah, he must be careful. He had been too long without a woman's love, and his control was not strong.

He must remember to confess his love, to ask her to be his wife, before he grew too carried away with his caresses. She must never think he was only trifling with her.

"Papa, may we go down one more time?" Alistair was asking, pulling on his father's arm.

"It is Melissa's turn, is it not?" Anthony asked distractedly.

"She and Miss Barnes have gone to the house. I saw them as we started climbing."

Anthony swung round, searching the white expanse between the hill and the house, and discerned the two figures almost at their destination. "Ah, I had not realized. Well, if the others are ready to return, we shall have one last ride, son."

"Thank you, Papa. I have had so much fun this afternoon."

"I have, too. It has been a good day, has it not?"

"Yes. Everything has improved since Miss Barnes came to us." Alistair paused and looked up at his father. "I don't ever want her to leave."

"Nor do I, son, nor do I."

Tonight, he promised himself, he would express those sentiments to Sarah instead of his son.

SARAH SLIPPED DOWN the back stairs to the kitchen, where all was activity, the servants hurrying to do the housekeeper's bidding.

"Are there any problems?" she asked the frazzled Mrs. Clayton.

"No, child. Everything is going as planned. I'm just so nervous, hoping all will turn out well. Are you sure you shouldn't be at the table, though?"

She referred to a decision Sarah had made when she returned to the house after the sledding. That morning one of the neighbours, a widower aged some seventy years, had sent his regrets because of illness. His absence gave Sarah the opportunity to remove herself from the guest list.

"I'm sure. We don't want the numbers uneven." The housekeeper nodded doubtfully.

"I'll just fix myself a tray and take it upstairs. I know you can't spare anyone right now."

"Very well. You are most considerate, Miss Barnes. Be sure to try the aspic that accompanies the roast. I believe it turned out well, thanks to your recipe."

"Of course I will," Sarah promised, even though she had no appetite. "Mr. Whitfield's neighbours will be quite impressed with his table this evening."

"What did Mr. Whitfield say about your not attending the dinner?" Mrs. Clayton inquired.

Sarah fought to retain her composure. She had not informed Mr. Whitfield of the change of plans. It did not matter what he thought, she decided firmly. It was not her place to attend an evening party.

"He said nothing," she said, moving towards the door.

"But he has insisted you be present at all the other meals since the guests arrived." Mrs. Clayton was watching her with sharp eyes.

"I think he was nervous about entertaining, but he has relaxed now, since you and the staff have done so well." She added, "You have noticed that Mrs. Myerson and Mrs. Scott are taking turns serving as hostess now. So I am no longer needed and have been returned to the schoolroom." She tried to make her voice light and pasted a smile on her face.

"But he owes you much, Miss Barnes. We could never have entertained guests properly if it were not for you," Mrs. Clayton insisted, warmth in her voice.

"I only guided you, Mrs. Clayton. You have done the work. Now, I shall retire to my room and leave Mr. Whitfield in your expert hands."

With another smile, she fled the kitchen and trudged up the stairs. The tears sliding down her cheeks fell into the soup, but it didn't matter.

CHAPTER NINE

ANTHONY STOOD AT the door of the parlour, greeting neighbours he hadn't seen since Larissa's death. Eighteen of those who lived nearest had been invited to join his guests this evening.

As he received them, he discovered that he was happy again. He no longer mourned for his wife. He had loved her, but somehow, in the past few days, he'd accepted that she was lost to him, that there was still life to be lived and that he could love again.

It was a dizzying feeling to be free at last of the lost feeling with which he had lived the past two years. And he owed it all to Sarah. He smiled particularly warmly at that thought and set Mrs. Comstock's heart aflutter.

"My, Mr. Whitfield, you are certainly in good spirits," she gushed.

"And why not, Mrs. Comstock? It is Christmas, after all, a time of love and magic." His gaze slipped from the elderly woman to the stairway where Sarah would appear.

"That it is, that it is. We are pleased to see you entertaining once more."

"Thank you."

As Mrs. Comstock passed into the room, along with her husband, Anthony signalled to Clayton.

"Yes, Mr. Whitfield?"

"What guests are we missing?"

"None, sir. Mr. Brandford sent his regrets this morning. It appears he is bedridden."

"I am sorry to hear it," Anthony said, his mind on another matter. "Perhaps you had better remind Miss Barnes of the hour. She seems to be late." His gaze was still fixed on the stairs, but when his butler did not respond, he turned to him, with a frown.

"Er, Miss Barnes is not dining with the guests this evening, sir."

"Why not?" Anthony snapped.

"She said with Mr. Brandford not coming, the numbers would be wrong. The missus and me assumed she'd talked to you."

"Well, she did not!" Anger welled up within him. He did not want to sit through a long evening entertaining without Sarah there. How dared she make such a decision without consulting him!

He dismissed his butler, knowing Clayton was anxious to continue with his duties, and perhaps to escape his master's anger. Relaxing his clenched fists, Anthony turned to his guests, but his heart was no longer in it.

He'd been so sure Sarah had responded to his kiss, that she felt something for him. Now his confidence was eroded. She was avoiding him, even at the risk of incurring his wrath, because she did not want to be with him. The joy of Christmas left him, and he wished his guests would disappear as quickly as his good spirits had.

Lord Abbott, seated beside him again at the dinner table, chided him for his silence. "Do you wish us all to vanish? Your guests are becoming uncomfortable."

Anthony straightened in his chair and glared at his friend, who had come too close to the mark. "What do you mean?"

"You know what I am talking about. You have been acting as if you wished us all to the devil." John's face softened as he added, "I have been pleased to see you so much in spirits of late. What has happened, Tony?"

Anthony fought the urge to confide in John. He could not do so. Instead, he made an attempt to brighten his expression and smile at his guests, ashamed of his self-indulgence.

"My apologies. I was blue-deviled, but it is no matter." He sipped his wine and then asked, "So, how is your courting proceeding?"

Miss Denison was seated at Lord Abbott's right hand, engaged in conversation with the vicar, and he sent a fond gaze her way before he responded. "Very well. I think we are of like mind."

The smile on John's face reminded Anthony of his own feelings before he'd realized Sarah was avoiding him. With a forced grin, he congratulated his friend.

"Oh, I have not asked for her hand yet. I should like her to see my home before I do so. I wondered . . . if we all might drive over to my place tomorrow for luncheon." As Anthony considered his request, John hurriedly added, "It is not quite an hour's drive. We would return before dark, and it would give your staff a rest."

"But the snow is too deep for the carriages, and I have only two sleighs. I do not believe they could carry all of us."

"I have two, also. I shall send for them in the morning. Will you agree?" John asked, leaning forward eagerly.

"Of course, John," Anthony replied. It was the least he could do for his friend. After all, it *was* Christmas.

ANTHONY ROSE early the next morning—at least, early for someone who had played host until long after midnight. He climbed the stairs to the schoolroom, sure he would find the elusive Sarah with his children.

"Good morning," he said as he entered the room.

Sarah sat at the table, Justin in her lap, Alistair and Melissa at the table. The children jumped up to greet their father. He was pleased to see them so much happier than they'd been a few weeks ago.

Sarah, however, did not demonstrate any pleasure at his appearance. He sat down across from her.

"Good morning, Sarah." When she only nodded, avoiding his gaze, he added, "Has Justin graduated from the nursery to the schoolroom?"

"No, Papa," his youngest responded. "Nanny Buckets doesn't feel well." Justin snuggled against

Sarah, a contented smile on his face, and aroused his father's envy.

"I am sorry to hear that. Do you need additional help, Sarah? One of the maids could—"

"No, sir. Justin is no problem."

"But our plans have changed. You cannot remain in the schoolroom all day." She still had not looked at him, and Anthony's fears were growing. Had his actions caused her to revile him?

"What do you mean?" she finally asked.

"We are to travel to Lord Abbott's home. It is not quite an hour away. His staff will serve us luncheon, giving the Claytons a rest, and then we shall return before dark." He watched as her hold on Justin tightened, causing the little boy to stare up at his beloved governess.

"I cannot accompany you, sir."

"Why not?"

He knew his blunt question did not please her, but he was too upset to be polite.

"Sir, there is still much to be done for tomorrow night's party, and someone must tend the children. They are my responsibility, after all."

"I have numerous servants capable of supervising my children, Miss Barnes," he insisted, reverting to formality in his anger. "Surely you do not think they will be harmed if they are out of your care for one afternoon?"

"No, of course not, but there is too much to be done."

"The truth of the matter is you do not care to go."

He wished he could take back his angry words. He did not want to confirm what he most dreaded to hear. For the first time since he'd stepped into the schoolroom, she looked at him, her eyes sad and distant.

"No, sir," she almost whispered, "I do not care to go."

Even though he wanted to insist on her presence, the fearful looks on his children's faces forced him to contain his anger.

"Very well. You may remain here. But you *will be* in attendance tomorrow evening."

"I cannot. I have no evening gown to wear." She laid her cheek on Justin's blond head and hugged the little boy to her.

"I do not care if you come in rags. You will attend the party. I refuse to go through another evening like last night."

"Did something go wrong?" Sarah asked, looking at him in surprise.

Yes, everything. You were not there. "No, of course not, but I felt the responsibility of entertaining alone. You were supposed to assist me. We shall find something for you to wear before tomorrow evening. But you *must* attend."

She did not argue with his pronouncement, but he was not sure she would cooperate. She seemed determined to cross him at every turn. Damn! He did not want to spend the day away from her. He wanted to cuddle her against him as she was cuddling Justin. He wanted to bring a smile to her lips, to caress... He stopped his thoughts at once before Sarah realized what he wanted, too.

"I should like Alistair and Melissa to join me for breakfast this morning," he said abruptly.

"They have already eaten, sir."

"Then they may eat again. All right, children?"

His clipped tones brooked no disobedience, and the two children slipped from their chairs, murmuring their agreement. The fearful looks remained on their faces, irritating him even more.

"They have been very good, Mr. Whitfield," Sarah said urgently.

"I am not going to beat them, Sarah! I only wish to enjoy breakfast with them." Not only did she not care for him, she thought him cruel to his children.

"Of course I did not think you would harm them, but your temper appears to be... a little uneven this morning."

He wanted to tell her that *she* was the cause of his uneven temper, but he realized that such an admission would be pointless at the moment. Instead he turned away.

"Come, children. Let's share a pot of chocolate together." He remembered his youngest. "Justin, you do not mind staying with Miss Barnes?"

The little boy only smiled at his father and pressed closer to Sarah, wrapping one little hand around her neck. *Lucky child,* Anthony thought, before he whisked the other two from the room.

Though Melissa clung to his hand as they descended the stairway, neither child said anything. Their little faces remained solemn, as if having breakfast with their father was an ordeal not to be anticipated. Had Sarah turned his children against him? Anthony wondered in a moment of irrational anger. No, of course not. She would never do such a thing. With a sigh, he requested Clayton to serve them something the children would like in the library.

"Why are we not eating in the dining-room?" Melissa asked in a small voice.

"Because we must talk, and I do not want to be interrupted."

Once the library door closed behind them, Anthony led them over to the settee. He intended to wait until Clayton had served them before introducing the subject that was closest to his heart. Melissa, however, said in a rush, "Please, Papa, do not send her away! We will be very good, I promise."

He frowned. "What are you talking about, child?"

"You are unhappy with Miss Barnes, but it is not her fault. I promise I will not tease Alistair ever again!"

Though he had not spoken, Alistair looked even more miserable than Melissa.

"I have no intention of sending Sarah away," Anthony hurriedly promised and watched as his two children relaxed. No, that was the farthest thing from his mind. Instead, he had hoped to manipulate his children to his advantage. Not an admirable thing, but he was desperate.

"Then why did you want to speak to us, sir?" Alistair asked quietly.

"Because I have encountered a small difficulty with your Christmas gift."

The two children looked at each other before turning to their father.

"What difficulty?" Melissa demanded.

"Well, you see, Miss Myerson does not like the country, so, of course, I eliminated her as your future mama. As you pointed out, Miss Scott talks strangely, so you did not care for her. That left only Miss Denison, but my friend Lord Abbott has fallen in love with her and wants to marry her. So, I am out of choices for your mama."

He expected to have to prod his children to suggest the solution that had occurred to him several days ago, even before he had kissed that solution. His children did not need any prodding.

After exchanging another look with her brother, Melissa exclaimed, "That is not a problem, Papa! We did not want Miss Denison."

"No? But then you will not have a mama."

"We have chosen someone else. We want Miss Barnes!"

Both children leaned forward, eager for his response, but that fearful look remained on their faces, as if they thought he would reject their suggestion out of hand.

"Miss Barnes?" he replied, feigning surprise. "Are you sure?"

Alistair, normally reticent, rushed in to defend their choice. "Oh, yes, sir. She would be perfect. We already love her, and she loves us. And she's lots prettier than Nanny Buckets."

His last remark, anxiously given, brought a quiver of laughter to his father's lips. "Yes, she is certainly prettier than Nanny Buckets."

Melissa could wait no longer. "Will you, Papa? Will you give us Miss Barnes for our new mama? Oh, please, Papa!"

He could hold out no longer. "If that is your wish, I shall certainly ask Miss Barnes to be your new mama." Both children launched themselves into his arms, and Anthony was glad he had not waited until they were served. Breakfast would have ended up on the carpet.

Once the children had resumed their places at the tea table, he cautioned them. "I shall ask Miss Barnes. That does not mean she will say yes."

"Why not?" Melissa demanded, alarm in her eyes. "She loves us."

"Of course she does, child, but perhaps she might not like to be my wife." Actual pain shot through his heart as he spoke his fears aloud.

"What can we do?" asked Alistair, ever practical.

"I do not know, son."

"I know," Melissa assured them. "We shall tell her how wonderful you are." She beamed at her father and then turned to scowl at her brother. "And this time you must help me, Alistair."

"Of course I shall help you. *This* is different!"

"What are you talking about?" Anthony asked, curious.

"Melissa wanted me to throw a snowball at Miss Denison, or spill my tea in her lap, to make her angry so she would not like us." Alistair squared his shoulders and stared at his father. "But I told her that would not be gentlemanly. Miss Barnes says I am to take care of ladies, not do bad things to them."

"Quite right, Alistair," he said, rewarding his son with a smile. Despite the amusement he felt at Melissa's crude plan, he turned to her sternly. "And you should not have asked your brother to do such a thing, young lady. It would have been most inappropriate."

"But it would have worked," Melissa muttered stubbornly. After receiving a warning look from her father, she mumbled her agreement reluctantly.

Clayton knocked on the door with a tray full of gingerbread and muffins, as well as a pot of chocolate. Their concerns relieved, the children fell upon the breakfast as if they had not eaten in a month. Anthony watched them, but his thoughts were on the woman upstairs. Yes, he would ask her. The question that remained was whether she would accept his proposal.

FROM THE WINDOW of the schoolroom Sarah watched the four sleighs pull away from the house. She had never had a sleigh ride. But honesty made her admit that it was not the lack of a sleigh ride that made her so unhappy. No, it was the prospect of not seeing Mr. Whitfield the rest of the day.

She might as well get used to not seeing him. Last night she'd written the service that had found her this position, asking them to assist her in finding a new one.

"Do you wish you had gone?" Melissa asked, slipping her hand into Sarah's.

"Oh, no, child, of course not. It is only that I have never ridden in a sleigh." She turned from the window and came back to the table, bringing Melissa with her.

"Papa will be glad to give you a sleigh ride, Miss Barnes. You have only to tell him," Alistair said. "He is most generous."

"Yes, I know he is. He did not—that is, when you went downstairs with him, he seemed disturbed about something. He was not angry with you?" In fact, the children had been in excellent humour since their return to the schoolroom. Sarah admitted to herself she was hoping to discover the reason.

"Oh, no, Miss Barnes. Papa would never treat us unfairly." Melissa assured her, her eyes wide, raising Sarah's suspicions. "He is a wonderful father."

"Yes, of course he is. Well, shall we practice your numbers? We have neglected our work the past few days."

"I would rather go sledding," Alistair pleaded.

"It was fun, wasn't it? But we cannot, dear. I am not well skilled in the art of sledding. I am afraid one of you might be injured and then I could not face your father." She expected further arguments, but both children, after looking at each other, immediately took out their slates to practise their numbers.

Sarah grew even more suspicious.

ANTHONY STARED up at the schoolroom window as the sleighs pulled away from the house. He thought he saw movement there, but he could not be sure. Probably it was the children and not Sarah watching his departure. Sarah had shown no interest in his movements since he kissed her among the trees.

Well, the week would soon be over. And after his conversation with the children, he was determined to confront Sarah upon his return. He suspected that by then John would have made his proposal to Miss Denison.

In fact, John had already informed everyone of his intentions simply by the seating in the sleighs. Anthony had Mr. and Mrs. Scott in his sleigh. The three Myersons occupied the second sleigh. Thomas was with Mr. Denison and Miss Scott in the third sleigh. The fourth sleigh contained only Lord Abbott and Miss Denison.

The girl's father had raised his eyebrows at the arrangement, but he had not protested. Not when there was the distinct possibility of catching a title.

Anthony had tried to reassure him of his friend's intentions without actually saying anything. Besides, there was no impropriety as long as the sleighs all remained in sight of one another.

How envious he was of John, though. He would love the opportunity of a sleigh ride with Sarah. However, it was for the best that he had not been granted his wish. He was discovering he had little restraint when he was alone with Sarah.

Just thinking of her brought a response that was embarrassing. And he seemed to do little but think of her. Now that he had his children's blessing, he could scarcely wait to offer her the role of their mother.

He mentally urged the horses to go faster. The sooner the visit was over, the sooner his torment would end. He hoped.

CHAPTER TEN

THE SNOW BEGAN just before luncheon was served.

Sarah joined the children in the schoolroom, where they dined on trays carried from the kitchen in order to save the staff extra work. The children were extraordinarily cheerful, but Sarah scarcely heard their chatter as she stared out the window.

By the time they realized their beloved Miss Barnes was not paying attention, the falling snow had changed into a near blizzard.

"Miss Barnes! Miss Barnes!" Melissa called, jumping up from her chair to stand in front of Sarah.

"Yes, Melissa?" Sarah finally responded, glancing at the child's impatient face.

"We have been talking to you and you did not answer."

"Sorry, darling. I was watching the snow."

Alistair ran to the window. "It is snowing even more than when we went to the woods."

"Yes, I'm afraid so."

"Will Papa be all right?" Melissa asked, her little face knotting into a frown.

"Yes, he will be fine," Sarah said, hoping she was right. "I am sure they will just stay at Lord Abbott's home until the snow has stopped."

Relieved of their worry, the children returned to the special biscuits Mrs. Clayton had sent up for dessert.

Sarah, however, had no interest in sweets. She was dismayed at how much her thoughts dwelled on Mr. Whitfield and how much she missed his presence. Her misery today portended a miserable future, when she would not even have the children as comfort.

She moved back to the window and stared out at the white, swirling snow. Her head seemed no clearer than the horizon, and her heart would remain frozen long after winter had disappeared, without the love she'd discovered in the Whitfield family.

"ANTHONY, don't be foolish. It would be senseless to venture out in this storm," John protested, catching his friend by the arm.

"John has the right of it," Thomas chimed in. "Can't see your hand in front of your face in that storm."

"My children will worry about me," Anthony protested, still not convinced.

"Miss Barnes will reassure them. You are fortunate to have someone like her."

"So you've told me, Thomas, time out of reason," Anthony muttered.

"Well, and I am right."

"I value Sarah more than you can know, Thomas. I do not need you to tell me of her sterling qualities." Nor did he need Thomas to keep reminding him of the real reason he wanted to return to Whitfield House this afternoon.

He knew his children would be safe and reassured. But he had been counting the hours, even the minutes, until he would see Sarah again, talk to her, explain everything to her. Now he would be stuck here for who knew how long.

"Do you think the storm will last long?" he asked, voicing his concern.

John shrugged. "Who knows? You know how unpredictable these storms can be. Do you remember the one about three winters ago that lasted for two weeks? Lord, I thought it would never stop snowing."

Anthony groaned.

Once the ladies were assured they would not have to brave the storm, they settled in contentedly in Lord Abbott's magnificent home. The servants scurried to prepare bedchambers and an impressive evening dinner for their lord's guests.

Sleeping gear was assembled from trunks in the attic and Lord Abbott's own closets, with the visitors' clothing to be refurbished while they slept. Every conceivable need was met—except, of course, Anthony's.

Nothing his host could do would whisk him back to his own home, his children and Sarah. He paced the salon where they spent the afternoon, ignoring entreaties to join in the charades, the card games, even billiards.

As day turned to night, he finally settled with a book in one corner of the room. Even should the snow stop tonight, he realized, he could not leave until morning.

After dinner, John took Anthony aside.

"I think I'm going to talk to Mr. Denison this evening."

"About what?" Anthony asked, his mind elsewhere.

"About marrying Claire, of course!" John exclaimed in irritation before looking around to see if anyone had overheard him.

"Oh, yes. Congratulations."

"Not yet. She hasn't accepted. That's when you congratulate me. What's wrong with you this evening, Tony?"

"My apologies, John. I shall extend my congratulations at the proper time, I promise you. You will let us know?"

"Naturally. I shall be unable to contain my joy."

John turned to cross the room to Mr. Denison's side and whisper in his ear. The two left the room while the others, except Anthony, were singing Christmas carols around the harpsichord.

A few minutes later, Anthony watched as Mr. Denison re-entered the room and drew his daughter from the group. Anthony sat in misery, wondering if *he* would have good news to proclaim after he returned to his home.

Only minutes later, the singing was forgotten as John and Miss Denison, followed by her father and several servants with bottles of champagne, returned to the salon.

Anthony raised the glass full of champagne supplied by a servant and wished his friend well. Now if only it would stop snowing.

AT THE WHITFIELD residence nothing was seen of the house party until early the next afternoon. The snow had stopped in the late morning, much to everyone's relief. After all, preparations for Mr. Whitfield's large party that evening were almost complete. It would be a shame to have no guests.

Sarah stoically set about her tasks, ignoring the longing in her heart. She was determined to keep herself hidden away during the party. The music, the laughter, the flirtations—they were not a part of her life.

"They've come back!" Melissa shouted, dashing down the stairs just as Sarah returned from a consultation with Mrs. Clayton.

"Melissa," she admonished calmly, though her heart had begun to beat like a drum, "ladies do not run or shout in a house."

"Yes, Miss Barnes," the child replied, but her grin remained as brilliant as before.

"Where is Alistair?"

"Jenkins said he could help clear the path to the stables." The smile vanished, replaced by a pout. "He wouldn't let me come."

"Of course not. Ladies do not—"

"I don't think I want to be a lady."

Sarah considered pointing out that ladies did not interrupt others, but she abandoned her teaching and smiled instead. "Never mind. You shall be first to greet your father."

"That is true!" Melissa exclaimed, her smile returned. "And I shall give him a big hug!"

The child continued toward the front door, but at a more decorous pace, and Sarah watched her with envy. Then, concerned that she might reveal her feelings, she scurried up the stairs and out of sight.

Only minutes later, a chambermaid found her inspecting the garlands decorating the upper hall.

"Miss Barnes. I've searched ever'where for you. The master wants you to come to the library."

Sarah gripped the bow she was straightening so tightly that it pulled loose from the branches. "I—I shall be there in a moment. I must repair the ribbon."

The maid hurried back to the kitchen. Sarah stared at the ribbon, trying to remember what she was to do with it. Her breath came in short gasps and her fingers trembled.

I should have departed before he returned. Impossible, she remembered. There was a blizzard. She reminded herself he probably only wanted to check on the arrangements for the party. Or to tell her his good news.

She swayed at the thought of his engagement to Miss Denison. It was what she had worked towards. Of course she would be happy for him. And the children.

Like a condemned woman riding to her death on the guillotine, Sarah dropped the ribbon and turned to walk in a stately manner down the stairs, staring in front of her but seeing nothing.

A footman opened the library door for her and she entered, stopping just inside. Mr. Whitfield stood looking out the window, his back to her.

"You sent for me, Mr. Whitfield? The preparations for the party are well in hand. I think—"

"I did not send for you to find out about the party," he protested, swinging around and striding across the room to her.

His nearness was even more disturbing than her thoughts had been. She stepped away from him, towards the settee.

"Everything went well while we were gone?" he finally asked.

She turned to answer and discovered he had followed her and was again at her side. She moved away. "Y-yes, of course. The children were concerned for your safety, but I reassured them."

"Thank you."

There was an awkward silence. Then Mr. Whitfield asked, "Have you heard the good news?"

She lowered her lashes, hoping to hide her pain. "No, but I would surmise I am to wish you happy?"

"Not me. John, that is, Lord Abbott. Miss Denison has accepted his offer."

Unable to look at him, fearful of seeing pain, or anger, or even despair, she whispered, "What will you do now? Miss Scott is ... is pleasant, or—"

When he said nothing, she risked a peep at him to find him scowling at her. She looked away.

"The children do not like her."

His abrupt dismissal of the only candidate left for the role of mama to his children left her bewildered. "But ... the children will be disappointed."

"Sarah," he began urgently, but when he closed the distance between them again, she backed several paces away. He halted at once, then asked, "Are you fearful of me?"

"No, of course not, Mr. Whitfield."

She risked another glance at him, but his expression had not changed from the ferocious frown he'd worn earlier.

Finally, in measured tones, he said, "I do not want to disappoint my children."

"Perhaps there are some young ladies in the neighbourhood, even attending your party this evening, who would suit."

"No, I can think of no one."

"Then what will you do? It is too late to return to Town to discover other eligible ladies." Sarah took another step away from him, as if she could distance herself from the pain his words brought her.

He suddenly walked away from her, returning to his earlier stance at the window. With his back to her, he said, "I know of only one female who will do."

"Miss Myerson?"

Laughing harshly, he turned to look at her. "No, not Miss Myerson. Whom will you suggest next? Nanny Buckets?"

"No," she murmured, wishing the interview would end.

"Have you no idea who the eligible lady could be?" he asked, walking slowly toward her, his hands clasped behind his back.

Though she could not explain it, she felt threatened by his approach. "N-no, I have no idea."

"It is you, Sarah."

Was it her heart beating so loudly? Sarah could hear nothing but an intense drumming. Her vision blurred, her head spun and her knees buckled. Before she sank to the carpet, however, Mr. Whitfield caught her in his arms.

He carried her to the settee even as she recovered, struggling from his grasp.

"I did not mean to so alarm you," he assured her, though he did not hide his displeasure. "Most young ladies receive a marriage proposal as a compliment."

"It is not possible..." Sarah whispered.

"My children will be greatly disappointed if you refuse. You have been their choice all along."

His children? Was it only for his children? How silly could she be? Of course he was asking her only for his children's sake. After all, as he said, there was no one else.

"You will have a comfortable home, three children who adore you. Many would settle for less." He returned to the window, and Sarah's gaze followed him, hungering for some crumb of encouragement, warmth.

Anthony stared out at the snow-covered ground, his heart colder than the frozen outdoors. He'd been so sure Sarah felt something for him. But every step he'd taken towards her had only caused her to back away. And she'd suggested every lady he'd ever met, and some he hadn't, as his wife. But never herself.

He feared he was losing the one person who had relieved his sorrow, brought desire and love to him when he thought he'd never feel them again.

That fear made him angry... and cold. So cold.

"I suppose, if you need time, I can wait for your answer," he said stiffly, afraid he would reveal his vulnerability if he were not careful. He held his breath as he awaited her answer.

Sarah knew what she wanted. She wanted to marry him, to be his wife, to love him... Her thoughts skidded to a halt. He had not mentioned any emotion. She must not expect too much. But she could not refuse the opportunity given her to remain near him, to be with the children. "No," she whispered.

"No?" he roared, spinning round. "What more do you want? Name it, Sarah. I *will not* disappoint my children!"

Though his words confirmed her greatest fear, Sarah did not change her mind. "I meant, no, I do not need more time. I—I will...if you are sure, I will marry you. For the children," she added, trying to protect her poor heart.

His anger slowly faded to the coldness Sarah had earlier noted. She shivered.

"Very well."

She did not know how to respond. She wished she could run to him, as Melissa had done, and feel his arms around her as they had been on the sled. And have him kiss her once more.

But they were marrying for the sake of the children.

"I—I should finish preparations for this evening," she finally murmured when he said nothing else, not looking at her.

"Very well," he repeated, staring out the window once more.

Sarah slipped from the room, tears welling in her eyes. She'd once dreamed of marrying, having her own home. Now it was to happen. She was so unhappy.

ANTHONY DID NOT turn round until he heard the door close behind her. He had hurried home, eager to see her, to talk to her, to ask her to marry him.

It had never occurred to him he would be even more miserable if she accepted him.

For the children. Those were her words.

His shoulders stiffened in determination. He would woo her. After all, she must not have too much distaste for him if she would agree to marry. He would show her the happiness they could have, if she would only let him. He would have to be patient.

But he would begin this evening when his neighbours gathered. He would introduce her as his wife-to-be.

He strode to the desk and sat down. Pulling towards him a piece of stationery, he wrote furiously. When he finished, he reread what he had written and gave a pleased nod. Then he rang for Clayton.

"Have this delivered to Miss Barnes at once."

When Clayton returned, Anthony was reclining in his chair, spinning daydreams of his perfect life once Sarah was installed as his wife to warm his bed, to love his children, to run his household smoothly.

"Miss Barnes asked that I bring this to you, sir," Clayton said.

Anthony raised his eyebrows. *She* was sending him messages? He took the missive and opened it. Only seconds later, he slammed his fist on the desk. "Damn and blast the woman! Can she not cooperate?"

Clayton took a step back. "Is something amiss, sir?"

"Yes! Everything!" He leapt from his chair and began pacing the large room. He had felt noble with his aim of gently leading Sarah into his dream of happiness. Now she was refusing to cooperate. "Aha! Send Mrs. Clayton to me."

"Begging your pardon, sir, but the missus is up to her neck in preparations for this evening. Is it urgent?" Clayton's fearful expression brought a twitch of humour to Anthony's lips. The poor man was caught between his master's command and his wife's ire.

"No, no, of course not. I would not disturb Mrs. Clayton. I shall tend to the matter myself. That will be all, Clayton."

The butler gladly retreated and left Anthony staring at nothing. Sarah thought she could refuse to attend the party, thought the excuse of not having a gown to wear would suffice. She was wrong. He would supply her with the proper clothing, and then she would do as he bade. He remembered his father saying, "Begin as you mean to go on." That was what he intended to do.

When he reached his bedchamber, he faltered for the first time. The door leading from his dressing-room into the mistress's bedchamber had not been opened since Larissa's death. Clearing his throat, Anthony forced himself to push open the door.

Mrs. Clayton must tend to the room regularly, he thought as he moved inside, because everything shone. Memories flooded his head as he noted the silver-backed brush Larissa had always used on her long blond tresses. The room was decorated in a gentle, feminine style, too sweet for his taste, he realized with surprise, but suited to Larissa.

It would not suit Sarah, he decided, but he would give her free rein to redecorate. He marched into the dressing-room and threw open several cupboards. They were filled to overflowing with expensive gowns. Larissa had needed a new gown every day, it seemed to Anthony. But he had been pleased to indulge her.

He threw at least ten garments over his arms, choosing ones in vibrant colours that would flatter Sarah. It amazed him that he could think of Larissa now as a fond memory. Only a month ago, he could not have entered this room.

His thoughts returned to his present task. He stared in dismay at the slippers and shawls, carefully stored. It was impossible to know what Sarah would want as accessories. He would tell her to make her own selection.

He unlocked the door that led to the corridor and ran up the back stairs two at a time to burst into the schoolroom. Only Nanny Buckets and the children awaited him.

"Where is Sarah?"

"She is helping Mrs. Clayton, Father," Alistair replied.

"We have said nothing," Melissa whispered, a delighted grin on her face. "When are you going to ask her?"

Nanny Buckets leaned forward, her deafness making it impossible for her to understand what was being said. "Eh, sir? What did you want?"

Anthony gestured silence to his children before shouting to the elderly nurse. "I am seeking Miss Barnes. Is she—"

"I am here, sir," a quiet voice said behind him.

He spun round to discover Sarah standing in the doorway. Warmth flooded him, giving him pause. Before he could say anything, she continued, "I've been assisting Mrs. Clayton, if you don't mind."

"You should be preparing for the evening's entertainment."

Her eyebrows arched over her brilliant blue eyes. "That is what I said, sir. I have been preparing—"

"To attend, my dear, not to serve."

His quiet interruption did not please her. Sarah stiffened her shoulders. "I have already explained that I shall not be attending, sir."

"Obviously I neglected to explain something vital to you, Sarah, my dear. *I* am master of my household, and I say you shall attend."

His triumphant smile faded as Miss Sarah Barnes, soon to be Mrs. Whitfield, calmly shook her head and replied, "No, sir, I will not."

CHAPTER ELEVEN

SARAH WATCHED as her employer's features stiffened. It was hard to think of him as her future husband, if, indeed, he was. It was possible he might dismiss her on the spot if his expression was anything to go by.

"You shall do as I say!" he snapped.

She failed to reply, knowing that to do so would only incite him to greater anger.

"Papa, are you and Mama—I mean, Miss Barnes, arguing?" Melissa asked tearfully.

Mr. Whitfield reassured his daughter, but Sarah stared at her in surprise. "You informed the children?" she demanded.

"You were their choice. Why should I not?"

"When did you tell them?"

Justin had begun to sniffle and whimper, distracting his father, but Melissa responded. "He told us before he went away, but we promised not to tell you. And we didn't, either, did we, Papa?"

Sarah felt indignation surge within her. He had discussed their marriage with his children before he discussed it with her! "Why did you not just write a note to inform me of my future, sir? Or perhaps it wasn't necessary to inform me at all! I would just follow orders whenever they were given!"

"Sarah, you are not being rational," he said, reaching out to touch her shoulder.

She stepped away from him, determined to retain her anger. It was a safer emotion than the longing that filled her whenever she was near him. "Rational? It is not rational to be angry that you presumed I would accept your offer? That you informed your children before you bothered to talk to me? Even a governess deserves some consideration, Mr. Whitfield!" She almost spat the last words at him.

"Why are you angry with Father, Miss Barnes?" Alistair asked, a worried frown on his face. "Don't you want to be our mother?"

"Eh? Mother? Whose mother?" Nanny Buckets demanded, her eyes lighting up with interest.

Sarah fell to her knees next to Alistair, the sight of his dear face diminishing her anger. "Oh, darling, of course I do. It is just . . . It is something adult, Alistair. You must not heed us."

She looked up to find Mr. Whitfield watching her. He no longer appeared angry. Turning to the nanny, he said in a loud voice, "Nanny Buckets, the children are to have a treat. Send for a maid and have something good brought up from the kitchen for them." He smiled at his two older children even as Justin clapped his hands and chanted, "Gingerbread!"

"You have both been very good at keeping our secret. Sarah and I have several details to discuss, but do not worry. She has agreed," he added softly, a finger to his lips and a meaningful glance at the nanny, who was distracted by Justin's antics.

Sarah could only smile weakly at the children's questioning looks, relieving them of their worries. He only told the truth, but she still could not believe it herself. How could she convince anyone else?

"Now, Sarah and I will go downstairs to finish our discussion."

He swept up the dresses he'd laid on the table and took Sarah's arm with his free hand. Before she knew what was happening, he had pulled her into the hall and closed the door behind them. "Come with me."

His autocratic order didn't appease her, especially after his previous high-handedness. "Of course, master," she replied in dulcet tones. Let him think he had the ordering of her. She would show him.

She rebelled earlier than she expected when he led her to the bedchamber that connected to his own. Mrs. Clayton had shown it to her once. She kept it in pristine state, as if the mistress had only gone on a visit. Sarah did not want to enter.

"We cannot go in there!"

"Why not?"

"Because . . . because it is your wife's bedchamber," she whispered, pulling against his hold.

"I do not have a wife...yet," he reminded her. "But we both know who will be filling that role. So it is only appropriate that we enter this chamber." Before she could protest again, he had pulled her inside and closed the door behind them.

"My reputation will be ruined if I am found with you in a bedchamber, with the door closed," Sarah protested fiercely.

"Then you'd best be quiet so no one will hear you," he replied, dumping the gowns on the large bed. "Come, look at these. Surely one of them will do for you to wear this evening."

Sarah had had little time to reflect, but the one thought that had survived her panic was that the man intended to ravish her. Faced with his concern over her wardrobe rather than her person, she stared at him in disbelief until her bottom lip began to quiver. Her mother had often warned her against her sense of the ridiculous. With her dramatic fears reduced to the mundane choice of a gown, she could scarcely contain her giggles.

When she made no move to look at the gowns, he turned towards her again. When he saw her face, he hurriedly stepped forward. "Sarah, you are not going to cry, are you?"

His concern only sheared the last of her restraint. "If I had any sensibility at all, I'm sure I should," she muttered between chuckles.

He towered over her, but her laughter relaxed the tension in him, too. "You always surprise me. What has set you off? I thought you were about to enact me a Cheltenham tragedy."

"And I thought you were about to—" The inappropriateness of their conversation brought her to an abrupt halt. "I beg your pardon, sir. I did not understand that you were concerned about my wardrobe," she added with a straight face.

Her eyes widened as he stepped closer. When she would have moved away, he reached out and caught her. He could not resist Sarah's warmth. Now that he'd tasted her lips, she had only to smile at him to light a fire within him.

Her laughter, and the thought of making love to her, drove all thoughts of wardrobe from his mind. "With your beauty, my dear Sarah, you have good reason to be on your guard," he murmured, showing his comprehension of her unspoken thought.

The nearness of him, the husky drawl of his voice, the smile that curled his lips mesmerized Sarah, and she made no attempt to dodge those lips as they moved to hers. Memory of their kiss in the snow kindled a fire in her, urging her to press against him.

His arms wrapped around her and hers encircled his neck, loving the feel of his hair between her fingers. His lips caressed hers, his hands warmed her, and Sarah could hardly remember anything, only the delight filling her.

"Sarah," he murmured, his lips moving to her neck as he lifted her from the floor.

"Sir!" she protested, suddenly frightened by his actions as well as by her own loss of control.

At once he released her and stepped back, and Sarah felt both abandoned and relieved, her cheeks flooding with hot colour. She could not look at him. He must think her wanton to give in to his touch so easily.

He crossed the room and stared out the window, saying nothing. Sarah would have run away if she'd thought her limbs would carry her, but she was shaking violently. When he spun around, she twisted her fingers tightly together, hoping to maintain some kind of composure.

"My apologies," he said briskly and gestured towards the bed. "Look at the gowns. There are others in the cupboard as well as gewgaws to match them. Help yourself to anything. I shall expect to see you at the party, where we shall announce our plans."

He moved towards his bedchamber, but when Sarah remained quiet, he paused at the door, though he kept his face averted. "I shall not apologize for what occurred, Sarah, but I will ensure it does not happen again."

His words did not please her. In fact, they caused her heart to shrivel in pain, but she would not show her emotions. "Sir, I shall attend the party on one condition."

For the first time since he'd held her, he turned to look at her. She raised her chin, determined to remain strong.

"You are insisting on conditions?" he demanded, his autocratic façade in place once more.

"Yes, sir. You must not announce our... our plans this evening. Your guests depart tomorrow or the next day. Please wait until they are gone. It will only embarrass and anger the Myersons and the Scotts if you do so."

He stared at her so intently she dropped her gaze. Finally, he answered, "Very well. You are right. I shall make no announcement this evening. But be sure you are in attendance, or I will drag you downstairs, dressed or no."

When the door closed behind him, leaving her alone in the dim room, Sarah collapsed on the bed. Drawing deep breaths, she gradually recovered her composure, but her thoughts remained fixed on the man who'd departed.

His promise to never touch her again only reminded Sarah of his reason for their marriage—his children. If not for them, he would never marry again, mourning his beloved Larissa.

Her spirits drooped. In spite of the attraction between her and her future husband, he appeared determined to keep his distance. Her only consolation was in knowing that he wanted her even if he would not take her. But that consolation would do little to warm the winter nights. She was to be a mother... but not a wife.

The rustle of silk as she wearily rose reminded her of the task before her. She had to appear this evening in one of his wife's outdated gowns. Though she abhorred the thought, she had no choice.

But she had also to make sure the gown was not too rich in detail to be inappropriate for a governess. She did not want the county gossiping about her and Mr. Whitfield now. There would be talk enough when she became his . . . his children's mother.

DAMN! Anthony leaned against the closed door, fighting the urge to swing it open again and take Sarah back into his arms. He'd almost lost control.

It was Sarah's fault. His mind had been completely on selecting the proper gown, but when he'd turned to find her laughing . . . well, the delight he'd felt had swiftly changed to desire.

She was so beautiful.

Larissa had been a beauty also, but she would have been in tears had he ordered her about in the tones he'd used with Sarah. He felt guilty at such a critical thought. Larissa had been a delight to protect, to care for, to enjoy. But she had never challenged him, never done battle with him.

A smile returned to his lips. Sarah would make conditions. Her courage in doing so, even though he was sure he had frightened her with his behaviour, made her all the more desirable. So much so that it frightened *him*. He'd desired Larissa, but he had never lost control.

He wanted to lose himself in Sarah, to fill her with his love, to never leave her bed. But he must await their marriage. And he had promised her he would do just that.

The special licence he had brought back from London with him was in his bureau drawer. He had wanted to ensure he could keep his promise to his children, so he had persuaded the bishop to leave the bride's name unwritten. He crossed the room to look at the licence as reassurance that his torment would not last long.

ANTHONY AGAIN stood at the door to the parlour greeting his guests. And again he watched the stairs for Sarah's appearance. Surely she would not ignore his wishes—nay, his orders.

"Where is Miss Barnes?" Thomas asked, stepping to his side from just inside the parlour. "She promised me a dance this evening."

Anthony gritted his teeth. He wanted to tell Thomas that all Sarah's dances were his. But he was being unreasonable. "She will be down soon. She promised she would attend."

More guests arrived and he welcomed them, wishing all the while that Sarah was at his side. He had begun his campaign to find a mother for his children, but now he wanted Sarah for himself.

He signalled to Clayton after his neighbours entered the parlour. "Miss Barnes should be—"

The sound of footsteps on the stairs drew his gaze. Unconsciously, he moved to meet Sarah as she reached the final step, extending a hand to her. The forest green silk gown was cut low, revealing her magnificent bosom. Then it flowed to the floor, swaying with her graceful descent. A patterned silk wrap accented the gown, and Sarah's auburn curls were tumbling about her shoulders enchantingly.

Drawing her hand to his lips, he caressed it as he wished he could her mouth. Memory of their earlier embrace flooded him with warmth. "Come. I'll have the musicians strike up a waltz."

"I cannot dance the first dance with you, Mr. Whitfield," she protested, slipping her hand from his.

"Why not?" he demanded, irritated by her constant refusal. "It is what I want."

"Then you would be going back on your word. You promised not to make an announcement tonight."

"All I suggested was a dance, Sarah."

She shook her head firmly, sending curls bouncing about. "You might as well make the announcement if I dance the first dance with you. It would be an insult to your guests. After the first dance, you may have your choice of ladies."

"You mean I must dance with Miss Myerson or Miss Scott?" he asked, outraged. "I will not."

"Then ask the highest ranking of your neighbours. But you cannot ask me for the first dance."

He arched his eyebrows as he stared down into her beautiful face. "Then what will you do?"

She looked taken aback. "Why, find a chair and watch the merriment, I suppose. Or dance should I receive an invitation. But I intend to do my best to fade into the background this evening. That is what a governess should do."

Anthony knew she was right. He did not want to cause talk among his neighbours, but he did not want to turn her loose, either. "Very well, but do not flirt with the other gentlemen if I do not have that right."

He knew he sounded overbearing, but he could not help himself. Expecting compliance, or even apologies, he was surprised when she raised her chin and smiled.

"Ah, we were talking of dances, sir, not flirting. That is another subject entirely."

Before he could even think of a response, she whirled from his grasp and entered the parlour.

By the time he reached the door, she was already within Thomas's clutches. The cad was escorting her to the punch bowl! Even as he returned to his post to greet new arrivals, Anthony vowed to himself that Thomas would know his plans before the night was finished. Sarah was *his!*

SARAH FELT most self-conscious in all her finery. She had selected the simplest of the elegant gowns and then stripped it of the lace and ruffles that had framed the bosom. In fact, she had had to enlist one of the maids to help her add the ruffle to the hem to make the gown long enough. The former Mrs. Whitfield had not had Sarah's inches.

Once she had entered the parlour and been greeted by Thomas Crutcher, she relaxed.

"I was afraid you would forget you promised me a dance," he said as he served her a glass of punch.

"Why, of course not, Mr. Crutcher. Though I wasn't sure you would remember once the ladies surrounded you." She smiled up at him teasingly.

"I've been hiding," he whispered. "Now that John's spoken for, it leaves only Tony and me."

Sarah looked away, biting her bottom lip. If Mr. Crutcher only knew, he stood alone as the available man. "Perhaps you should circulate. There are many charming ladies here this evening."

"Later, perhaps," he said with a shudder. "First, I must have my dance."

Only minutes later, Mr. Whitfield entered the parlour and signalled to the musicians, at the far end of what was normally the morning-room, to begin play. The servants had opened the two rooms and removed the rugs and furniture to allow many couples to participate.

Sarah watched as Mr. Whitfield led out the vicar's sister, an elderly spinster, as his first partner. She smiled at his choice. He was determined to avoid his young guests.

She and Mr. Crutcher joined in the country dance at the other end. Her partner was an excellent dancer, and she found herself swept up in the movement. It had been several years since she'd danced, and she loved it.

They moved down the line of dancers until they came face-to-face with Mr. Whitfield and his partner. Sarah smiled at them both, but she missed a step. Hastily she turned her thoughts away from him, smiling at her own partner in apology. When she looked back, Mr. Whitfield was frowning ferociously in her direction.

Unable to comprehend his displeasure, she put it aside. She never seemed to please him, be it in his arms or attending his guests.

The music ended and Mr. Crutcher offered to fetch her another glass of punch. "I'm afraid we may have overtired you with all our merrymaking, Miss Barnes. Your cheeks are quite flushed."

"Thank you, Mr. Crutcher, but I must visit the kitchens to talk with Mrs. Clayton. Thank you for the lovely dance. You are quite skilled. I am sure some of the other ladies would enjoy your escort."

She turned and found herself next to a young lady she'd met at the church several times, a Miss Bethany Graham. In no time at all, she had introduced the two and heard Mr. Crutcher solicit the young lady's hand for the next dance.

Well satisfied with her work, she slipped from the room, after noting Mr. Whitfield standing with the vicar, his sister and several other neighbours.

In truth, there was little to be done belowstairs, but Sarah had wanted to retire for a few minutes. How could she hide her feelings from the man? She'd longed to be in his arms during the last dance, but if he had no desire to touch her again, then she could not let him realize how much she wanted him to do so.

With a sigh, she entered the kitchen.

Only a few minutes later, she headed back to the party, firm in her resolve to maintain an attitude of indifference. She would avoid Anthony this evening, fading into the background as she had told him. He would be fully occupied with his neighbours.

Her gaze swept the room as she slipped past several gentlemen conversing at the door. When she espied the squire in conversation with Mr. and Mrs. Myerson, Sarah felt safe. Nevertheless, she hurried to the other side of the room, where the vicar was standing, to ask him about the local charities. He would provide extra protection from her husband-to-be.

"My dear Miss Barnes, it is so kind of you to be concerned. I was telling Mr. Whitfield earlier about your generosity since you moved here."

"You were discussing me, Reverend?" she asked faintly.

"Well, actually, Mr. Whitfield commented on how good you were with his children. He was quite intent on praising you himself, without any assistance from me."

"How . . . how kind of him."

"Yes, wasn't it?" a deep voice asked behind her.

Sarah whirled round, face-to-face with the one person she'd thought to avoid. "Mr. Whitfield! I did not—I thought you were conversing with Mr. Myerson."

"So I was. However, it is time for the next dance, and I have come to claim my partner."

Sarah looked about her, hoping to discover another lady standing near. However, the hand that grasped her arm left her in no doubt whom he meant.

"Come, my dear. By chance, the musicians are going to strike up a waltz. Isn't that a coincidence?"

He nodded to the vicar, who smiled benignly at the pair of them, and led Sarah to the centre of the floor.

CHAPTER TWELVE

"YOU MUSTN'T..." Sarah hissed as his arm came around her.

"It is not the first dance. I have done my duty, as you pointed out. Now I may please myself."

She looked up at his face, determined though handsome, and swallowed her protest, relaxing to his touch. She had danced the waltz only a few times, but she loved the graceful steps. Now, enveloped in Anthony's embrace, she discovered an excitement she hadn't felt before.

"Did you enjoy your dance with Thomas?"

"Yes, of course," she replied, keeping her gaze fixed on Anthony's cravat. "He is a fine dancer."

"I am also accounted to be a fine dancer."

She peeped at his face. Surely he could not be jealous? "As you are, Mr. Whitfield. Very fine," she murmured faintly.

"Don't you think it would be proper to call me Anthony, or Tony, when we are alone? After all, we are to be married."

"Shh!" she cautioned, fearing he might be overheard. "I do not consider us to be alone in the midst of a hundred people, sir."

"It is the only way I dare."

"I beg your pardon?" Sarah asked, not under-standing his words.

He swung her round, pulling her closer than was strictly proper. "Never mind. I have a special licence, so we may present the children a fait accompli before Christmas."

Sarah swallowed. She hadn't realized the marriage would take place quite so swiftly.

"You have no objections, do you?" he demanded, drawing back so he could see her face.

She dipped her chin lower. "No, no, of course not," she replied breathlessly.

"And will you object if I ask Thomas to remain with us for Christmas? He has no family to visit."

"Of course not. I enjoy Mr. Crutcher's company."

"Humph. Then perhaps he should visit John in-stead."

She looked up at his disgruntled expression. "Why? I truly have no objection."

"I know," he replied, staring at her. "Never mind, we shall work out something." He pulled her close once more and moved around the room.

Sarah wanted the music to last forever.

LATER THAT EVENING, in the library, after the guests had either departed or retired to their bedchambers, Anthony and his two friends sat by the fire, sipping a glass of brandy.

"Well, the week has come to a close, Tony. Have you chosen a bride?" Thomas asked, bringing up the very subject Anthony had intended to discuss.

He hadn't known exactly how to make his announcement, but his friend had made the way clear. "Yes. Yes, I have."

"Not the Scott chit, I hope," John said lazily. "She acts about ten years of age. Much too young to mother your brood."

Before Anthony could answer, Thomas said, "No, of course not, nor the Myerson girl, either."

John arched his eyebrows and looked at both men, but Anthony stared at Thomas and asked, "How do you know?"

Thomas raised his glass in a salute. "Because you're no fool."

Anthony stared at his friend, trying to read the expression on his face. "But I promised my children a mother for Christmas."

"Haven't said you didn't," Thomas agreed with a smile.

"But if he doesn't choose one of the three ladies he invited, who will it be?" John asked. "After all, Claire is to marry me, and you have already dismissed the other two."

Anthony remained silent, watching Thomas, who laughed. "You are so besotted with your Miss Denison that you cannot see what is before your very eyes," Thomas answered.

"And what have *you* seen?" John demanded, leaning forward.

"That Tony will marry Miss Barnes."

"Is it true, Tony?" John asked.

"Yes." He turned to Thomas. "You have no objection?"

"Objection? She was my choice early on."

"Yes, that is what concerned me. I shall not stand aside for you, Thomas, though I value your friendship." Anthony tensed, waiting for his friend's response.

"Stand aside? What are you talking about?"

"She is mine. I will not surrender her to you."

Thomas roared with laughter, then said, "Why not, Tony? You made no protest when John here claimed Miss Denison."

Anthony said nothing, but John asked, "Are you in love with Miss Barnes, too, Thomas?"

"No, but this nodcock thinks I am. Right, Tony?"

Though Thomas was grinning from ear to ear, Anthony saw nothing humorous in the situation. "You were always telling me of her virtues."

"Course I was. I was trying to give Cupid a nudge."

Anthony sagged in his chair, relief filling him. He did not want to lose his friend. "Perhaps you should have been more concerned with the state of your own heart, my friend. John and I shall both have wives soon, and you will be alone."

"Yes, Thomas, you should be thinking of taking a wife, as well," John agreed.

"I am."

His two friends looked at him in surprise.

"I met a young lady this evening. If I may visit one of you for a little longer, perhaps I shall have an interesting announcement to make, too."

"Now that I know you have no wish to pay court to Sarah, you may visit as long as you wish," Anthony assured him, smiling.

"Perhaps you had best come to me," John said. "After all, Tony is planning to marry at once. I shall still be a bachelor for a few more weeks."

"Very well. Tomorrow, I will move to John's," Thomas agreed. "You and your bride will not want to be entertaining guests."

Anthony only hoped Sarah agreed. He wanted her all to himself. Visions of their wedding night filled his head.

SARAH WATCHED the carriage drive away, carefully following the cleared driveway, edged with banks of snow. The last of the guests had departed, though Mrs. Myerson had delayed her leavetaking until all the others had gone.

Sarah admitted her behaviour had been cowardly. Since the party two nights ago she had done her best to remain hidden both from the guests and Anthony. Miss Denison had sought her out to bid her goodbye with the hope of meeting her again when she returned as mistress of Lord Abbott's home. Sarah had assured her she would be happy to see her.

The others' goodbyes had been brief. Their disappointment occupied their minds, she was sure. Mr.

Crutcher and Lord Abbott had gone as soon as Mr. and Miss Denison had departed.

"But I thought you were going to remain with Mr. Whitfield through Christmas, Mr. Crutcher?" she asked as he bade her farewell.

"Nay, he will be too busy for guests," he replied with a wide grin. "But I shall see you once before Christmas." The wink he gave her left her in no doubt of his meaning, and she flushed.

Fearful of not controlling her emotions, she had decided the schoolroom was the best place for her. Now she no longer had any excuse to hide from Anthony Whitfield.

"They've gone," Melissa chanted as she ran into the schoolroom.

She would have difficulty returning the children to any sort of routine after Christmas, Sarah thought ruefully, until it occurred to her she might not have the teaching of them, after all.

"Miss Barnes, Papa said we may join you at luncheon in the dining-hall. Shall we go down?" Alistair asked, having followed his sister into the room.

A protest died on her lips. She did not normally eat in the dining-room. At least she had not before the advent of their guests. But as mistress of Whitfield House, she would be expected to do so. "Yes," she said, drawing a deep breath, "let us go down to luncheon."

Justin was left in the nursery with Nanny Buckets, but Melissa and Alistair each took Sarah's hand and led their precious Christmas gift downstairs.

"The house is so much nicer with just us, isn't it?" Melissa asked, swinging Sarah's hand. "I was very tired of smiling at all those people."

"Is smiling so difficult, then?" Sarah teased. "You do not seem to be having much difficulty with it today."

"No, of course not. We have received our wish. You will be our new mama, just as we asked. Didn't we, Alistair?"

Sarah looked down at the silent boy holding her other hand. His grey eyes, so like his father's, were fixed on her as he answered. "Yes, that was our wish. You do not mind, do you, Miss Barnes? You do not mind being our mama?"

Sarah squeezed his hand. "No, darling, I am honoured to be your mama."

"Shall we call you Mama?" Melissa demanded.

"If you wish. Or you may even call me Sarah." She added the last for Alistair's benefit. After all, unlike Melissa, he remembered his mother.

"I shall call you Mama," Melissa announced blithely before turning loose Sarah's hand and running down the stairs ahead of the other two. "I'm going to tell Papa."

"And you, Alistair? What will you call me?" She stopped and waited for his answer.

His gaze returned to her face, filled with love. "I should like to call you Mama, also."

Sarah knelt and hugged him to her. "I am glad." He wrapped his little arms around her neck and returned her embrace.

"I believe I shall have to call you out, Master Alistair, for trifling with my future wife," his father intoned in his deep voice, interrupting their hug.

Alistair withdrew from Sarah's arms and giggled, an unusual sound from the solemn child.

"Father, you are teasing me. She is to be my mama. I am *supposed* to hug her."

"Ah. Right you are. My mistake." With the grinning Melissa holding his left hand, he extended his other to the two of them. "Will you join us?"

Alistair took Sarah's hand in his again and pulled her down the stairs to his father's side. Sarah shyly held out her free hand to Anthony but was unable to suppress the delicious shiver that ran through her at his touch.

He gave no sign of having noticed her reaction. "Shall we go in to luncheon now? It will be nice just being family, will it not?"

"Oh, *yes,* Papa. I am so tired of guests," Melissa replied dramatically.

"Cut up your peace, did they?" Anthony teased her, winking at Sarah.

"We were so afraid you might like one of those other ladies better than Mama," she explained to her father. "That was before we met them, of course," Melissa earnestly assured Sarah. "We loved you, no matter who came, but we were not sure of Papa."

Sarah could think of nothing to say in response.

After they were seated at the table and the first course served, Alistair interrupted the silence. "Papa, when will you be wed? Christmas is only three days away," he reminded them. "If she is to be our mama for Christmas, then you must marry her soon."

"Accurate as always, Alistair. I have a special licence, and we may be married whichever day we choose."

"Today, today!" Melissa shouted gleefully.

Three eager faces stared at Sarah, awaiting her response. "T-today?" she repeated faintly.

"Yes, why not?" Anthony asked. "If we are going to marry, it might as well be today."

"But I have nothing to...to wear, nothing prepared. We cannot—"

"You may wear the gown you wore to the party. You appeared...to great advantage," Anthony finally said, a warm look in his eyes that she wasn't sure she understood. "As for preparations, I'm sure Mrs. Clayton can set forth a wedding supper without too much notice. We have only to summon John and Thomas, and the vicar, of course, and the deed is done."

"I do not—"

"You do still want to marry me, do you not, Sarah?"

His voice was low and gentle, his gaze caressing, and she could not have denied him if her life depended on it.

"Yes," she whispered, her eyes never leaving his.

Both children sprang from their chairs to hug Sarah, shouting their happiness.

"You have certainly pleased the children," he assured her, a smile on his face.

Ah, yes. The children. She had almost forgotten.

SARAH NERVOUSLY clutched her prayer book and stared at her reflection in the cheval glass. As Anthony had suggested, she wore the forest green silk gown. She'd added a halo of holly made that afternoon, its red berries and green leaves a festive touch to her wedding attire. Perhaps Anthony would not like it, but she thought it appropriate, since she was a Christmas gift.

Her only jewellery was a gold locket that had belonged to her mother. It fell to the shadow of her bosom, revealed by the décolletage of the gown.

"Oh, Mama," Melissa gasped as she slipped into Sarah's bedchamber. "You look beautiful!"

"Do you think so, Melissa?" Sarah desperately needed someone's approval. How she wished her mother were here with her.

"Oh, yes." The child walked slowly around Sarah, studying her with awe. "Papa will love you so much!"

Tears pooled in Sarah's blue eyes, but she refused to let them fall. Melissa was wrong, but she would not tell her. Anthony was intent on pleasing his children. His reasons for marrying her had everything to do with love for his children and nothing at all with love for her.

"Oh, I almost forgot. The vicar's sister, Miss Bonner, is below. She asked if she could be of assistance. She came with him to be at your wedding."

"How kind of her. Why don't we go down? There is nothing to wait for." Sarah didn't want to be closeted with the other woman. She feared there would be questions for which she had no answers.

They were to be married in the chapel attached to the house. It was seldom used nowadays, since a fine new church had been built in the village over a hundred years ago. Even Anthony's first wedding had been performed in the church. But on that occasion he and his wife had invited everyone in the county.

Sarah and Melissa went downstairs to discover only Miss Bonner waiting for them.

"The gentlemen are in the library, celebrating your nuptials with spirits, as gentlemen do," she explained with a raised eyebrow.

"Ah." Sarah could think of nothing more to say.

"Is Alistair with them?" Melissa asked.

"Yes, child, your brother is with your father. I am sure you must be very excited to receive a new mama today."

"Yes," Melissa said with conviction, but she pressed against Sarah.

"Are we to notify the gentlemen when we are ready?" Sarah finally asked, wondering about the correct procedure.

"Yes. Will you go into the chapel? I shall let the gentlemen know you are there."

Sarah turned to walk down the long hall, Melissa at her side, only to discover the Claytons waiting for her.

"Me and the missus just want to wish you happiness, Miss Barnes," Clayton said, a smile on his wrinkled face.

Mrs. Clayton wiped away a tear and then hugged Sarah. "We're so happy for the master and you. Everyone says to wish you well, miss."

"Thank you, Clayton, Mrs. Clayton."

Clayton stepped forward and swung open the chapel door for her. Sarah entered and felt a rush of tears. The chapel was dimly lit with many flickering candles, the nave lined with greenery and bows. It was as beautifully decorated as the parlour.

"Oh, Clayton, how lovely!" she exclaimed.

"'Twas the master's orders, miss. He said as how you would like it."

She blinked furiously to hold back the tears. "It is beautiful."

She and Melissa walked forward to stand in front of the candles. When she heard the door open behind her, she turned slowly round to look at her soon-to-be husband.

Anthony stopped on the threshold of the chapel, John and Thomas behind him. Sarah stood outlined in candlelight, a holly wreath on her glorious curls, the shimmering silk gown cascading to the floor. He thought he had never seen a more beautiful sight.

His mouth went dry and his knees trembled. He had thought of Sarah as his children's mother, as his lover, as many things. But he had never quite comprehended that she would be truly his, to share every part of his life.

"Papa, why are we stopping?" Alistair whispered.

"I was just admiring your new mother," he whispered.

"She is beautiful, isn't she?" Alistair agreed.

"More beautiful than anything in this world."

Murmurs behind him reminded Anthony that his guests were waiting, and he walked down the narrow aisle to where Sarah and Melissa, with the vicar's sister nearby, awaited him.

He took Sarah's hand in his and lifted it to his lips. She shivered as he caressed her skin, and he smiled deeply into her eyes. Her trembling lips, full and tempting, drew his gaze, and he fought against his rising desire.

"Well, shall we begin?" the vicar asked.

Distracted by Sarah's gleaming shoulders in the candlelight, he didn't hear the vicar's question until it was repeated.

"Do you have the special licence, Mr. Whitfield?"

"Oh, yes, of course. It is here in my pocket." He reached inside and drew forth the piece of paper that would make his dreams come true. How young men bore the weeks needed to call the banns for a normal wedding he did not know.

"Yes, all is right and proper. Very well. Join hands with your intended, please, Mr. Whitfield."

He took Sarah's trembling hand in his, squeezing it gently to reassure her. Her gaze flickered to his before falling away, her cheeks blooming with red.

"Dearly beloved, we are gathered here..."

As the vicar droned on, Anthony's gaze never left the bowed head beside him. He could think only of her. In just minutes, she would be his wife.

Tonight, she would be his.

CHAPTER THIRTEEN

FOR THE FIRST TIME since she'd left home after her mother's death, Sarah had someone to assist her as she prepared for bed that evening.

Polly, the girl who had received the promotion to lady's maid to the mistress of the house, beamed at Sarah's every request. Though Sarah asked little, Polly rushed to do each task as if it were of the utmost importance.

As she helped Sarah with her plain cotton nightgown, Polly giggled. "Glory, Miss Barnes—I mean, Mrs. Whitfield, it's hard to believe. Everything's happened so fast."

"Yes," Sarah murmured, unable to voice the confusion that filled her.

"I'll just brush out your beautiful hair now," Polly said, indicating the chair for Sarah.

"No." Sarah tried again, realizing how sharp her reply was by Polly's bewildered expression. "No, Polly. I shall brush it myself. I—I am unused to assistance, you know. Tomorrow evening we shall—you may—I need to be alone now."

"Oh, yes, miss, of course, I'll leave you be." With a quick curtsy, the girl sped from the room.

Sarah sank down on the bench in front of the mirror with a sigh of relief. The wedding supper had gone on forever, long after the children, ecstatically happy, had been sent to bed. The vicar had grown expansive, talking about his parishioners, and John and Thomas had told her anecdotes about Anthony. Her new husband had sat at the other end of the table and said little. His gaze, however, had remained fixed on her.

The longer he stared at her, the more nervous she became. She knew she could be a good mother to his children. But there were so many other duties involved in being his wife. And in everything she did she would be compared to his first wife.

The wife he loved.

She drew the hairbrush through her long hair, staring unseeingly at her image. A movement reflected in the mirror broke into her thoughts and she spun round, her eyes wide.

"You look like an angel," Anthony murmured. He was leaning against the door that connected their two rooms, as if he had been there for a long time.

Sarah stared in fascination at his open-necked nightshirt, discreetly covered by a silk robe. Suddenly she realized she was clothed only in her nightgown. She hurried to the bed and struggled into her robe before facing him again.

"I—I did not hear you knock."

One eyebrow arched and he straightened to his full height. "I did not knock. You are my wife. It is proper for me to visit your room."

Sarah immediately remembered the kiss they'd shared the day of the party. She looked away. "Was...was there something you wished to discuss?"

"Discuss?" He took several steps forward.

His movement drew her back to face him. "Surely that is why—"

He froze, his gaze burning into her. Then he took another step forward. "I am here because I am your husband."

When Sarah didn't respond, her eyes growing wider, he said harshly, "You are my wife. As husband and wife, we—"

"But...but you promised..." Sarah whispered, struggling to understand what was happening.

"What? Don't be ridiculous!"

"When you...when you kissed me, you said it would not happen again." Sarah's thoughts were confused. She wanted him to kiss her again. But not when he loved his first wife. Not when he did so because it was his duty.

"I meant not until we were married!"

"But you married me because of your children. You wanted a mother for them!" Sarah gulped in air, trying to control her rising hysteria.

"Does being a mother preclude being a wife? I did not hear vows of motherhood this afternoon. I heard only marriage vows."

Sarah stared at him, her lips pressed together to still their trembling, tears filling her eyes. She had come to love her husband, as well as his children. She wanted to be a wife in every way. But she wanted so much more. Filled with confusion, she looked away.

Anthony stared, his gaze never leaving her. When she finally dared look at him again, his expression had grown remote. The emotion in his eyes was that of distaste, which only gave her greater pain. Finally, he spoke, his voice filled with icy disdain. "I shall not disturb you again."

Tears rushed down her pale cheeks as he strode from the room. "Wait!" she called, but the word came out in a whisper and her husband did not hear her.

He slammed the door behind him.

BLOODY HELL! She was his wife!

Anthony fumed as he paced his large bedchamber. The bedchamber he had not expected to occupy this evening.

In his fantasies, he'd seen himself content, holding his beautiful new wife in his arms, lying among the bedclothes, lost to the world. It seemed he had forgotten to explain his plans to Sarah.

She thought he had married her only to provide a mother for his children. As his anger and frustration eased, he thought back over his dealings with Sarah. Perhaps he had led her to believe—certainly the children were his main concern. At least, they had been until Sarah had joined his children as the most important people in his world.

She was young, inexperienced. She did not understand the hunger that drove a man. He pictured her as she'd stood in the chapel, the candlelight gleaming on her smooth shoulders and breasts. The golden locket flickering in the candlelight as she breathed, urging him to touch—

A soft knock on the connecting door interrupted his thoughts. He turned and stared at the wood as if it could answer the questions that flew through his head.

"Yes?" he demanded harshly, not moving.

"Please, Anthony, may I...may I speak with you?"

He walked slowly to the door, then swung it open. She stood in front of him, her head bowed, those glorious auburn curls falling like a curtain to shield her face from his view, her white cotton robe and gown as pure as the snow outdoors.

Fighting the overpowering urge to draw her to him, he stood stiffly still. "Yes?"

Her head came up slowly, her eyes large pools of confusion and indecision. "I—I offer you my apologies. I am prepared to do m-my duty as your wife."

Duty. He had pictured passion, wanting, sweetness, even love. He hadn't thought of duty.

"No." He hadn't meant to speak so harshly. The sudden pain that filled her eyes before she swiftly hid it told him he'd been cruel. "'Tis not necessary, Sarah."

His fingers tightened on the door until they were bloodless as he waited for her response. He wanted her to beg, to plead, to insist. He wanted her to want him. As he wanted her.

Without another sound, she turned and walked back through the dressing-room that separated their chambers, back through the open door, closing it behind her. Shutting him out. Leaving him alone.

He let the door slip from his grasp and it swung to. His bride. His gift to his children. Again he paced the floor, but this time it was determination that drove him, not anger.

The children had won their Christmas wish. Now he would make his. He would wish that the Christmas angel in the next room would love him, as she loved his children.

And he would do his part to make the wish come true.

SARAH WAS NO COWARD. Though she was tempted to ask for a tray in her room the next morning, she forced herself to descend the stairs for breakfast.

The children would not be there to provide a buffer between her and her new husband. As she came down the stairs, once more wearing her traditional grey gown, she lifted her chin and looked serenely around her. She would not reveal the trembling that shook her insides.

Clayton beamed at her as he escorted her into the breakfast-room. "Good morning, Mrs. Whitfield. The missus has prepared a special breakfast for you this morning."

"Thank you, Clayton, but she should not have gone to so much trouble." Especially when Sarah had no appetite.

Clayton ignored her words and left the room to return almost at once with a hot pot of tea. Then he stepped to the hall doorway and motioned to some unseen servant.

"Is all well this morning?" Sarah asked, wondering what could be so urgent on this quiet morning.

"All is perfect, madam," Clayton assured her. "I'll just bring up your breakfast." He went down the stairs, leaving her alone.

Almost at once, the door to the hallway reopened and Sarah was joined by her new husband. Rather than the disgruntled frown she expected, Anthony's smile was warm as he rounded the table. To her surprise, he touched her shoulders and bent to place his firm lips against her cheek.

"Good morning, Sarah," he murmured before seating himself next to her at the head of the table.

"G-good morning."

He busied himself pouring a cup of tea and passing it to her, then did the same for himself. "Did you sleep well?"

His genial question made Sarah wonder if she had dreamed the difficult scene last evening. And it also made her want to pour her cup of tea on his head. Of course she had not slept well. It had taken hours to calm herself. Then she had dreamt of the man!

"Of course. I slept beautifully, thank you. The bed is most comfortable." She happened to look at him as she spoke of the one piece of furniture that dominated her bedchamber, and she could not keep the blood from rushing to her cheeks.

"Yes, it is."

A subtle reminder that he, too, had occupied that bed at various times. But not last night.

Clayton came back into the room, much to Sarah's relief, accompanied by several footmen with trays. As their breakfast was served, Sarah looked everywhere but at Anthony. He graciously thanked the servants when all was ready, and they left the room.

"Come, Sarah, you must eat a hearty breakfast. We have much to do today."

"Do?" she said in confusion. What did he mean?

"Yes. As soon as you are ready, we shall go into town. Unless, of course, you have completed all your Christmas shopping. *I* certainly have not."

Sarah's gaze flew to his and then away again. Shopping. She had made gifts for the children and the Claytons, but she had nothing for her new husband.

"Even if you have, I'm afraid I must demand your presence. I insist on ordering you some new gowns this very day. I do not want to see you wearing that horrid grey ever again."

She stared down at the offending gown and then back at him. "But...but I have no money for—I mean, the gowns are perfectly adequate—"

"I think you have forgotten your marriage yesterday, Mrs. Whitfield. Those gowns may be adequate for a governess, but you are now my wife. We have a certain social position to uphold, you know." His tone turned pompous, quite like the vicar's, and his eyes twinkled, inviting her amusement.

Her lips quivered, but she said, "Truly, sir, it is not necessary."

Anthony's amusement disappeared, to be replaced by a warmth in his gaze that caused her to tremble. "Yes, it is necessary. I *want* you to have pretty gowns."

"I could remake your wife's gowns," she offered. All her life she had scrimped and made do. She could not change overnight.

Anthony grasped her hand, which rested on the table, and carried it to his lips. "No, my dear Sarah. Do what you will with those gowns. Give them to the poor, to the servants, whatever you choose. But my wife does not wear hand-me-downs."

Stunned at his dismissal of what he had treasured for two years, Sarah stared at him.

Anthony dropped his serious air. "You must eat at once. The children are to accompany us, and they were up hours ago. I fear they will be stuffed with gingerbread if we do not hurry."

Sarah obeyed his command, more confused than ever. She had expected anger, sorrow, some emotion to show his disapproval of her behaviour last evening.

Did his happy spirit mean he did not care that she had not welcomed him to her bed? Was he pleased that he slept alone?

THE SMALL TOWN was bustling with business as folks hurried through the snow from one shop to another, making last-minute purchases.

Sarah, tucked snugly under a fur rug, her husband's arm round her shoulders and two children on the other side, had no interest in leaving the sleigh. It was her first sleigh ride, and she loved it.

"Here is Mrs. Chadwick's," Anthony announced. "She is the local dressmaker, you know. In the spring, if you like, we shall go to London and you may select more stylish gowns. But for now I want you to have something besides grey to wear."

She nodded, prepared to purchase several gowns to please him.

"Wait here, children, while I escort your new mama inside," Anthony ordered with a smile.

"Please, that is not necessary," she assured him.

"Oh, yes, it is."

She discovered why several minutes later as he gave strict instructions to the shopkeeper, much to the woman's delight, insisting his wife needed an entire wardrobe of at least a dozen gowns, slippers, shawls, nightclothes—which drew a blush from Sarah as he glanced her way—and anything else she desired.

Unable to protest in front of strangers, she sent him a speaking look that he greeted with a smile. "The children and I shall return for you in a little while, after we do some shopping for Mrs. Clayton. She gave us a list."

"But I should assist you."

"No, you should obey your husband, my dear wife," he assured her, gently chucking her under the chin before striding from the store.

"Oh, Mrs. Whitfield, he is such a handsome man," Mrs. Chadwick murmured, giving her an envious look.

Yes, he was, Sarah agreed, but much too puzzling to understand.

When she left the shop almost two hours later, she was wearing a bishop's blue wool gown that Mrs. Chadwick had had on hand and had hastily fitted to her. As she stood, undecided, at the door, her new finery covered by her old cape, inadequate against the cold, Anthony and the children arrived in the sleigh.

"Finished? Ah, I believe I see a different colour beneath the cloak," Anthony murmured, a bright smile on his face.

"Mrs. Chadwick had this gown already available. I thought you would prefer I do away with the grey as soon as possible."

"You have followed my wishes perfectly, Mrs. Whitfield," he assured her, bowing low before he assisted her into the sleigh. The two children giggled at his play-acting.

Before Sarah realized what he was doing, he had sent the sleigh flying along the narrow street, and then across the countryside towards Whitfield House.

She had not had a chance to shop for presents. She had nothing for her husband. Frowning, she tried to figure out a gift for him.

"Not enjoying the sleigh ride?" he whispered in her ear.

"Oh, yes. I love it!"

"Ah, I'm glad." He drew the sleigh to a halt in front of the house. After assisting Sarah and the children out of the sleigh, he nodded for them to go into the warm house.

Just as Sarah reached the steps, she was startled to feel something hit against her back. She spun round and sent crystals of snow flying everywhere. The explanation rested in her husband's hands as he stood beside the sleigh.

"You—you threw a snowball at me?"

"It's one of our traditions," he assured her gravely. "Every new family member must be christened in such a fashion."

"And if they join the family in August?"

"Oh, that's not allowed. Only during snowy weather."

The smile on his lips was growing larger every minute, and Sarah did not need the children's protests to know he was teasing her. She carefully retraced her steps until she was near him.

"I see. Are there other traditions I should know about?"

He pretended to think. "No, I don't believe so."

"Ah. Then perhaps we should start a new tradition." Quick as a wink, she scooped up a handful of snow and dashed it into his face.

Even as the children cheered and she turned to escape into the house, his strong arm captured her, pulling her to him. "Retaliation is not proper, Mrs. Whitfield," he assured her, brushing off snow with his other hand, "but since you have begun this new tradition, I must do my share."

Sarah tensed for more cold snow. Instead, without warning, Anthony's lips covered hers in a kiss that was anything but cold. Sarah sank against him as he clasped her tightly to him. All else faded from her consciousness. There was only Anthony, her husband.

He lifted his head, Sarah didn't know how much later, and murmured, "Welcome to the family, Mrs. Whitfield."

Her lips moved, but nothing came out. She was trembling and disoriented, shaken by the desire that filled her.

"You are cold. I should not have thrown snow on you with that thin cloak." He swept her into his arms and carried her up the steps to the door, immediately thrown open by the waiting footman. The children marched along behind them, cheering their father's action.

Sarah's spirits lifted. Perhaps Anthony did not long for his dead wife, after all. Wrapped in his arms, her lips still tingling from his touch, Sarah made her own Christmas wish.

CHAPTER FOURTEEN

AN AIR OF OPTIMISM seemed to fill the house, at least in Sarah's mind. She spent a pleasant afternoon with her new family, preparing for Christmas.

Justin joined them from the nursery and sat upon his father's knee while Sarah, with the help of Alistair and Melissa, wrapped the gifts they had purchased for the servants. Anthony entertained all of them with his teasing.

"Mama, may we have more gingerbread with our tea?" Melissa asked as she placed her finger on the bow Sarah was tying.

"I don't know if Mrs. Clayton has any more made," Sarah replied. "*Someone* has eaten a great deal of gingerbread the past few days." She smiled at her family, filled with contentment.

"It was Father," Alistair whispered loudly.

"I protest, Master Alistair," Anthony said with exaggerated hauteur. "I believe you have eaten your share."

"But you're bigger, so you must have eaten more," his son replied before covering his mouth with his hand to hold back a giggle.

Everyone joined in the laughter.

"Well, we can be sure your new mama didn't eat too much gingerbread," Anthony said as the laughter died down.

"Why, Papa?" Melissa asked.

"Because I carried her into the house. Too much gingerbread and I wouldn't have been able to lift her."

Sarah protested, setting off another round of laughter.

Tea was served with a plateful of warm gingerbread. At the sight of it, the children burst into giggles, leaving Sarah to thank Clayton and assure him the children were pleased.

After the butler had withdrawn, Alistair, his mouth full, of gingerbread, sighed and said, "This is the best Christmas ever."

Melissa agreed. "Thank you, Papa, for giving us Mama."

"It is my pleasure," Anthony murmured, and his gaze met Sarah's. The light in his eyes only encouraged her optimism. Perhaps she was being too greedy, but Christmas was a time for miracles.

As she dressed for dinner, she warmed her heart with the remembrance of Anthony's look. It spoke of more than gratitude for his children's happiness. As with the kiss, that look only concerned the two of them.

She wore the second dress the dressmaker had had immediately available. It was a pale blue gown, cut low with long sleeves and a high waistline. Matching slippers peeped from under the flowing skirt. Sarah had never had so many new clothes at once. But then, she had never occupied such a prestigious position. Nor had she ever hoped to. After her disastrous courtship, she had accepted her fate in life, that of servant to others.

Anthony had rescued her from such a sad life, had given her three children to love, a beautiful home and lovely gowns. And she wanted more. So much more. She wanted her husband to love her.

He was waiting for her at the bottom of the stairs, and his approving gaze swept over her new attire. She felt her cheeks heat up and her body tingle in response to him. She longed for the right to throw herself into his arms, to beg for another kiss. Instead, she sedately completed her descent to place her hand on his extended arm.

"You appear to great advantage this evening, my dear," he said, and patted her hand.

"Thank you, Anthony."

Dinner proceeded with mundane conversation, each saying nothing important, but Sarah feared her gaze gave away her desire each time she looked at him. Certainly his eyes were filled with more than the pleasantries they exchanged.

"Is all in place for tomorrow? It is Christmas Eve, you know," Anthony reminded her.

"Why, yes. I believe so. The church carollers will appear, to accept your gift for the poor. We shall attend the Christmas Eve services at midnight. Christmas Day there will be a feast for everyone in the house. And the next day we shall distribute the gifts to your tenants."

"Only my wife for two days, and already you have everything well in hand. You are wonderful, Sarah."

She was absurdly pleased. "Thank you, Anthony, but your staff takes care of most things."

"Do not be so modest, dear Sarah. Since you took over my household several weeks ago to help me entertain, everything has improved."

"I only—thank you, Anthony," she finally murmured.

It was hard to believe that it was only a little more than two weeks ago that he had come to the schoolroom with his proposal that the children select their new mama. Then she had scarcely known the man sitting opposite her. Now her happiness rested in his hands.

He joined her in the morning-room for tea, forgoing the tradition of drinking alone. Sarah took up her needlework, grateful for something to occupy her hands. She had only a little left to do for the collar she was making for Mrs. Clayton.

In fact, all her gifts were finished except for this small task and a large one that loomed before her. She still had nothing to give her new husband for Christmas.

Ever since their return from town, she had worried over a gift for him. She had only one more day to prepare. The idea of embroidered handkerchiefs had been dismissed, but she could think of nothing else.

"What are you working on so industriously?" he asked as he sipped his tea.

"A gift for Mrs. Clayton. I am almost finished."

He frowned. "You could have bought something to give her while we were shopping today. It is not expected that you make all your gifts, Sarah."

"But it would not be from *me*," she said quietly. "I can scarcely believe that I am ... am your wife, much less feel free to use your money to purchase gifts."

He set his teacup down and stood to tower over her. "You *are* my wife, Sarah, and will be my wife, God willing, until I die. What I have is yours."

She could not look up at him, but kept her gaze firmly fixed on her work. "Thank you, Anthony."

Nothing more was said for several minutes. Anthony, instead of sitting down again, prowled about the room. Finally, he injected a lighter note into their conversation. "I promised the children we would go sledding again tomorrow. Do you think you will feel up to such strenuous activity?"

"Oh, yes, I shall enjoy it." Her cheeks flushed as she remembered her last outing down the steep hill with Anthony.

"Good."

When Sarah finished her needlework, she gathered it up and stood. "I believe I shall go to bed now. I shall need to be up early to get everything accomplished in the morning if we are to sled in the afternoon."

"Very well. Good night, my dear," Anthony said, halting her as she passed by him and kissing her on the cheek.

She looked at him and then away again, afraid he would see the longing in her eyes. "Good night," she whispered, and hurried from the room.

It was only after she reached her bedchamber that she could not find her thimble. Thinking she had probably dropped it as she left the morning-room, she retraced her steps.

She did not find it before reaching the morning-room door, so she opened it and slipped inside, preparing to explain to her husband why she had returned. Instead, she stood silently watching him as he toasted the large painting above the mantel.

"Dear Larissa, I love you so much. I shall never stop loving you, or the children you gave me."

With her heart broken, Sarah fled the room, shutting the door behind her ever so quietly. Her foolish dreams were shattered, her hopes dead. He would not, could not love her, because he still loved his first wife. He had married her for the sake of his children, as he had always told her.

With tears streaming down her cheeks, she sought the privacy of her bedchamber, but its richness mocked her. She would have preferred the hardier confines of the governess's chamber. At least there she deserved what she received.

As she lay on the bed in her misery, she sought ways to rectify the mistake she had made. Finally, it came to her. She knew what to give her husband for Christmas.

ANTHONY SIPPED from the glass of brandy with which he had toasted his dead wife. Then he looked up at that serene face again. "But you are not here, Larissa. And I have found love again. I know you will not begrudge me my happiness. She is a good mother to your children. And a joy to our lives.''

He did not say the words he hid in his heart, that Sarah would make him even happier than his first wife. Larissa had been his childhood sweetheart. But she had never stirred his senses as Sarah did. She had never made him strive to do better, as Sarah did every day. No, he could not say those words aloud, even to Larissa's picture. It somehow seemed disloyal. But in his heart, he knew Sarah was a match for him in every way.

And soon, he promised himself, he would prove to her that they were a match in bed. But he would be patient. He would wait until she, too, felt the desire, the need, that flooded him each minute of the day... and night.

With a sigh, he downed the last of his brandy and left the room. It was almost Christmas. Perhaps the Christmas Angel would give him his wish.

SARAH ROSE EARLY the next morning. She thought she might as well get up, since she had been unable to sleep. But with her decision, there was a serenity, a sad, aching serenity that came from knowing what she had to do.

She hurried to the morning-room, asking Clayton to bring her tea there. With a sketch pad and charcoal, she began making the Christmas gift she would give to Anthony. Before she went away.

By the time she joined her husband at luncheon, she had accomplished a great deal. Her lack of sleep was catching up with her, but she put on a bright smile, hoping to hide her unhappiness.

"Sarah, is all well?" he asked at once, proving how little she succeeded.

"Why, of course. It is wonderful. Tomorrow is Christmas, you know," she chattered. "Have you presents for the children? They are so excited."

"I have given them the greatest present of all," he reminded her, warmth in his gaze.

But she knew now that that warmth was for his children, and not for her, as she had so wrongly hoped. She smiled and changed the subject.

Towards the end of the meal, he asked, "Are you sure you feel up to sledding today? The children will understand if you need to rest this afternoon. After all, much falls on your shoulders."

"No," Sarah said fiercely. She was determined to have this one last afternoon of happiness with those she loved. "No," she repeated more calmly, "I am looking forward to sledding with the children. If you have other things you must do, I am sure I can manage with the servants' help."

"Not at all. I, too, am looking forward to the sledding," he assured her, a teasing look on his face. "After all, I would never pass up an opportunity to cuddle with my wife."

Her cheeks flamed but she said nothing. If she spoke at all, she might betray her feelings.

In spite of the cold and snow, the sun shone brightly that afternoon. Sarah went down the hill a number of times, frequently wrapped in her husband's arms.

There were no more stolen kisses, but she revelled in his strength and closeness.

Justin was allowed to join the fun today, and she and Anthony took turns holding the little boy in front of them. He squealed with glee as they zipped down the slope. Alistair and Melissa romped and threw snowballs while awaiting their turns. They were equally willing to go with Sarah as with their father, though she did not go quite as fast.

When they trooped back to the house, Sarah was able to send the children to the nursery with a clear conscience, knowing they had enjoyed their afternoon. She immediately went to her own bedchamber to continue working on the gift for Anthony.

Since the two older children were to join them at the midnight services, Sarah allowed them to dine downstairs with the adults. Their presence kept her from facing Anthony alone.

"When will the carollers come, Papa?" Melissa asked for the tenth time as she munched the roast Mrs. Clayton had prepared.

"In about an hour, sweetheart."

"But you said the same thing the last time I asked."

"That's because you only asked five minutes ago," Anthony told the child with what Sarah felt was remarkable patience.

The difference in his behaviour towards his children now and two weeks ago was considerable. It consoled her when she thought of her departure. The children would miss her, but they would have their father.

She was the only one who would really suffer, and she believed she deserved to do so. It was her own greediness that forced her to leave. She wanted more than a good home, more than wonderful children, more than security for the rest of her life. She wanted Anthony's love.

"Sarah?"

Looking up, she discovered her husband and children staring at her. "I beg your pardon. I was distracted. Did you ask me something?"

"Yes, my love, I did," Anthony responded with a warm smile, and her heart cringed at his false words.

"Papa wondered if you were ready for dessert to be served," Alistair explained. He eyed the door that led to the kitchen with longing. "I heard we were having a syllabub."

Sarah smiled at the dearly loved child. "Right you are, Alistair. And I am particularly anxious for your opinion of it. It is an old family recipe." She picked up the small bell and rang it, and Clayton immediately appeared. "We are ready for dessert, Clayton."

He bowed and disappeared, only to return seconds later with the dessert. Sarah was not bothered with any more questions as the two children concentrated on the syllabub.

When it had been pronounced superb by the others, Sarah led the way from the table to the parlour, where the Christmas tree awaited them.

Anthony strode to the fireplace. "Ah, it is here."

The children and Sarah looked at him expectantly.

"The yule log, of course. Isn't it huge?"

Indeed, the fireplace was filled with an enormous log, thick as well as long. Sarah stared at it, knowing she would be gone long before it burned itself out.

"It will be a lucky year, with such a fine yule log . . . and because Sarah has become part of our family." Anthony stared at her, that warm look in his eyes again. She looked away.

"Come, Sarah. I want you to help me light our yule log, the first of many for our family."

"Had you rather not wait until it is truly Christmas? It is only a few hours." She looked at the children, counting on them to agree.

"No, Mama, we want to celebrate now, because we have you," Alistair assured her, taking her hand in his small one and tugging her up and towards his father.

"I anointed this log with my best brandy, Sarah, so that it will flame brightly. I am taking no chances on it dying out, though I should not worry with you as our luck."

He rang for Clayton, who arrived with a torch that he lit by holding it to one of the candles on the wall. Handing it to Anthony, he stood to one side, a smile on his face. Sarah heard the shuffling of feet and turned to discover the entire household staff had quietly entered the room.

"Thank you, Clayton," Anthony acknowledged. He then took Sarah's hand in his and carried it to the torch held in his other hand. "Light the fire, Sarah, my love, that this year and those that follow will bring health and happiness to us all."

Sarah stared into his grey eyes. She wanted to hide from the eager, smiling faces, the faces that wished her well, the faces that believed she would be with them to celebrate every year. But there was nothing she could do. She took the torch in trembling hands and stood before the huge log.

"May God bless the Whitfields and all who reside here," she said in a low voice. As she touched the torch to the log, it burst into flames and her audience raised a cheer. At once, a deep voice in the back began singing "God Rest Ye Merry, Gentlemen," and soon all had joined in.

Anthony turned his children and Sarah towards the others, his arms around the three of them, and he sang along. Melissa and Alistair stared in round-eyed wonder. Sarah, too, watched, as best she could through the tears.

CHAPTER FIFTEEN

As THE CAROL came to a close, a distant chorus could be heard.

"Ah, the carollers have arrived. Preparations, Clayton," Anthony instructed, though his words were unnecessary. One footman hurried to the front door to open it for the singers. The others hurried to bring forward the hot punch and sweet cakes that were ready for the visitors.

Anthony led the children and Sarah to the staircase, instructing the two little ones to climb several of the steps and be seated where they could see everything. He kept Sarah by his side, taking her hand in his and holding it to his chest.

The carollers hurried inside, glad of the warmth, and filled the hall with the music of the Christmas season. Words of hope, joy and love floated on the air, and Sarah's heart felt leaden with despair.

When the singers had ended their songs, enjoyed the repast provided, and accepted the gifts for the poor that Anthony gave them, they traipsed back out into the cold. The servants, after jovial salutations to the carollers, cleared the debris from the impromptu party.

"It is almost time to leave for the church service," Anthony announced to his family. "Melissa, Alistair, are you sure you will be able to remain awake?"

"Oh, yes, Father," Alistair said in spite of a small yawn he tried to hide. "We do not want to miss any part of Mama's first Christmas."

"Very well. Hurry upstairs and fetch your wraps."

He kept a hold on Sarah's hand even though she, too, turned to fetch her cloak. "No, my dear, not yet."

"But I must—"

"Come with me."

He led her into the morning-room and then instructed her to close her eyes. Sarah did as she was told, but she could not imagine his reason. Then the softness of fur brushed her shoulders and her face. Her eyes flew open.

Anthony had wrapped her in a beautiful, fur-lined velvet cloak, its colour a royal blue. "It matches your eyes and will keep you warm," he whispered before leaning forward to caress her lips with his.

Sarah stared at him in shock. "But I cannot—"

"Of course you can. It is your Christmas present, Sarah. You must accept it for the children's sake."

Sarah's smile faltered. Ah, yes, for the children's sake. If she was to give them this one last day of happiness, she must accept his gift. For the children's sake.

"Thank you," she whispered, staring at the carpet.

"It doesn't please you?"

"It is incredibly beautiful," she assured him, but still did not look at him. "I have never owned anything so...so elegant."

He started to speak again, a frown on his brow, when a call from Alistair stopped him. "Come. The children are waiting."

Melissa squealed over the beauty of her father's gift, and Alistair told Sarah she looked fine as fivepence. She smiled her thanks but said nothing. Feeling Anthony's eyes upon her, she urged the children forward to the waiting sleigh.

Anthony and Alistair assisted their womenfolk into the sleigh and then settled in themselves, one on each side. It was a tight squeeze, but Anthony slid his arm around Sarah's shoulder, to make more room, he assured her.

They set off at a quick pace, the sleigh bells jingling in the frosty night air. The snow took on a silvery hue through the shadows of the trees, and their world shrank to those inside the sleigh. Sarah hugged the moment to herself, to treasure the rest of her life.

After the celebration at the church, they returned to Whitfield House. Both children fell asleep on the way, leaving only Sarah and Anthony to see the light snow begin to fall, drifting slowly to the earth, to mingle with the white all round them.

When they arrived at the house, several footmen came out to carry in the sleeping children. Anthony turned his attention to Sarah.

"Come, my dear. Christmas is here."

"Yes," Sarah agreed painfully, staring up at him. "Christmas is here."

He frowned at the look on her face, but she darted past him into the hall. Before he could stop her, she hurried up the stairs and into her bedchamber. Laying the exquisite cloak upon her bed, she did not bother to warm her hands by the fire. Instead she opened a cupboard and took out a small packet wrapped in paper.

It was time to give her husband his gift.

ANTHONY WATCHED Sarah escape up the stairs. Something was bothering her, but he didn't know what. Several times this evening when she should have been happy, he had noted a strange sadness about her.

He paused by the door of the parlour and stared at the Christmas Angel atop the tree. He had hoped his wish would be fulfilled this special night, but clearly his wife was not ready to accept his love.

He would be patient.

After bidding the servants a Happy Christmas, he climbed the stairs to his own bedchamber. He surrendered his cloak to his valet's waiting hands.

"Go on to your chamber, Amos. I can dress myself for bed tonight. You have had a long day."

"Nay, sir, I do not mind."

A knock on the connecting door to Sarah's bedchamber brought both men to an abrupt halt. Hope flamed in Anthony's heart and he again dismissed his manservant. This time Amos made no protest, slipping from the room.

Anthony hurried over to the door and opened it. There was no blushing bride awaiting him. Sarah looked at him with pain in her eyes, tears on her cheeks.

"My dear, whatever is wrong?" he asked with concern, reaching to draw her to him.

She backed away and shook her head, saying nothing but thrusting a package into his hands.

"What is this?"

"Your Christmas present," she gulped before turning and fleeing back to the safety of her bedchamber.

Though his first inclination was to pursue her, Anthony paused and stared at the mysterious package in his hand. Slowly he unfolded the paper and stared at the exquisitely executed miniature of Larissa. It was a copy of the painting that hung over the mantel in the morning-room.

He walked back to his bedside, where candles burned, to better examine his gift. Had Sarah painted it? It was beautifully done, but why would she give him a painting of his first wife?

Lifting the miniature from its wrapping, he discovered a note folded beneath it.

"Dear Anthony,
My Christmas gift to you is this painting of Larissa, your greatest love. I also give you your freedom. I should never have accepted your offer of marriage. I thought I could be happy with a marriage of convenience, but I cannot.

The children adore you and will accept my departure. I pray that you will all be happy.

Love, Sarah

Pain rocked him as he realized he was losing her. His

wish would never come true because she would not be his wife. He crushed the letter in his hands, the prospect of divorce looming before him. Divorce? Never. Not in his family. He would insist— He stopped. Could he bring himself to force Sarah to remain his wife, to be unhappy?

He thought of her beautiful face this evening, tears on her cheeks as she lit the yule log. No, he could not cause her more pain. Sitting down heavily on the edge of his bed, he struggled to smooth the wrinkles from the letter, the only letter he had ever received from Sarah.

She could not be happy with a marriage of convenience. He frowned more deeply. He had never intended to offer her a marriage of convenience. It had been Sarah and not he who had rejected a greater intimacy.

The surge of anger that thought brought faded away as he studied the note. Did that mean she wanted more? That she wanted a true marriage? Then why was she leaving? What had caused her to give up hope?

As if sleepwalking, Anthony rose and walked to the connecting door. He crossed the dressing-room and, without knocking, opened the door to Sarah's bedchamber. There were only a few candles lit, and at first he couldn't see her. Then he realized the miserable lump in the middle of her bed was Sarah, sobbing amidst the blankets.

He silently moved to the bedside. "Thank you for my present."

At his first word, she froze, stifling her sobs in a vain attempt, he supposed, to hide her misery. He smiled gently, wanting to urge her into his arms, to comfort her. Instead, he remained standing.

"You are welcome." Her whisper was strangled.

"Are you quite determined to leave?" Her misery gave him hope.

"Yes. Yes, I am leaving in the morning."

Still she did not look at him.

"Ah. It would mar the holiday for the rest of their lives if you left the children on Christmas Day. Could you not postpone your departure?"

One eye peeped up at him tragically and he schooled his features to a pleasant smile.

"I—I suppose I could wait until the next day," she whispered, turning her head away from him.

"Oh, dear, that is a problem. You see, Mrs. Clayton was counting on your assistance then. Surely you would not repay her hard work with abandonment."

This time she turned to stare at him, the eyes less tragic, tempered with a rising anger. "Very well. I shall stay for one more day to—to assist Mrs. Clayton." Not turning away, she added firmly, "But I must leave the day after."

"Well, of course I would not want to delay your departure, but I do believe the day after will be the Lord's day, Sunday. Surely you could not break your marriage vows on Sunday?"

Now she sat bolt upright, frustration stiffening her spine and drying her tears. Ah, his beloved Sarah, strong and determined.

"Perhaps, sir, you will name the day that will be convenient for me to leave, since you do not care for my suggestions!"

He put one finger to his lips and pretended to consider her words. "I suppose I could . . . but I will not," he finished, abandoning his casual air. "Because it will break my heart when you leave."

Sarah's cheeks suffused with colour and her eyes widened. Then she turned away from him again. "Do not be ridiculous. It will not matter to you."

"You are my wife, Sarah."

"One easily replaced. There are many who will accept a marriage of convenience." Her voice was cold and hard.

"I never offered you a marriage of convenience."

Her head snapped up and she stared at him.

"You are the one who refused my attentions," he reminded her. She looked away. "Why, Sarah?"

"I did not expect—I am unwilling to—you love Larissa!"

He frowned, staring at her accusing look. Finally, he said, "Of course I love Larissa. She gave me my three children. I shall always love her." He noted with satisfaction the despair that filled Sarah's eyes. "But she is no longer my wife, and she is no longer my first love."

She knelt amongst the bedclothes, her auburn curls rioting about her beautiful face, hope building in her eyes, and Anthony had never seen such a humbling sight. His passion increased tenfold and he ached to take her in his arms. "Sarah, my dearest, I have fallen in love with you and will love you forever, as long as you will let me.''

"How... how do I know you are being truthful and not just saying so to persuade me to stay?"

He sat down on the bed beside her and reached out to caress one blushing cheek. "I cannot prove my love unless you will give me time."

"How much time?" she whispered, her cheek rubbing against his hand, her gaze fixed on his face.

"I shall need at least fifty years," he whispered in return, leaning closer. He reached for her and slowly pulled her into his embrace, his mouth descending to hers.

When he lifted his lips, she was lying in his arms, her own wrapped about his neck, a dreamy expression on her face. "Fifty years?" she whispered.

"At least," he murmured, kissing her brow, her cheek, wishing to touch every inch of her body. But he must not frighten her.

"Very well," she agreed, so calmly he almost missed the significance of her words. "But I am not sure I can give you more than fifty years, so you should not waste time," she said, even as her hands occupied themselves at untying his cravat.

He drew back in astonishment. His first wife had submitted to his lovemaking, but Sarah, his beautiful Sarah, had surprised him again. *She* would be a willing participant, giving him joy, pleasure, and, most of all, love.

"You... you love me?" he asked, suddenly hesitant.

"Of course I love you, Anthony. I would never have agreed to marry you had I not."

"You loved me even then? But you rejected me."

"Not really. I was shocked by your presence in my bedchamber. You talked only about the children. I had no idea you had any interest in me as your *wife*."

"Good Lord. We have already wasted several days, my Sarah. You will have to add them to the fifty years, because I refuse to give up even one day or night of loving you."

Sarah made no protest as he drew her to him. In fact, she assisted him to make up for lost time.

"MAMA! Mama! May we enter? It is Christmas morning!"

Sarah opened one eye and then blushed to encounter the amused stare of her husband. His arm tightened, pulling her closer to him, and she snuggled against his broad chest.

"Well? Shall we let the heathens disturb our morning?" he whispered. "Or just pretend we do not hear them?"

"They will arouse the entire household if we do not answer," Sarah whispered in return.

As the banging on the door continued, Anthony called out, "One moment, children. Be patient."

After a surprised silence, Melissa's small voice said, "Why is Papa in Mama's room?"

Sarah's cheeks burned and Anthony grinned, quite pleased with himself and his blushing bride. "I don't think my daughter is ready for that explanation," he whispered.

"Mothers and fathers do that sometimes," Alistair explained to his sister, his hoarse whisper reaching his parents.

Softer whispering followed, indistinguishable to Anthony and Sarah. He slipped from the bed and rummaged in Sarah's cupboard until he found her white cotton wrapper. "I think we shall have to order you something in silk," he murmured, holding it for her as she shyly slid from under the covers.

Before she could tie its ribbons, he turned her around and placed one last kiss on each bare breast, then returned his lips to hers. When he finally released her, she said, her voice husky with passion, "But then, I might never get dressed."

"I know. But I only have fifty years. I don't want to waste any time." They smiled at each other in perfect contentment.

"Father?"

"One moment, Alistair," Anthony repeated before whispering to Sarah, "I must dress. Wait for me."

Several minutes later, he strode through the door while slipping his arms into a jacket. Sarah had hurriedly donned a warm wool morning-gown. "Very well, you may enter," he called. The children burst into the room, giving equal hugs to both adults. Anthony swung Justin up into his arms, and Sarah took the hands of the other two.

"Shall we go see if Father Christmas left presents?" Anthony suggested.

"Yes, Father, but we have already received the best present of all," Alistair reminded him.

"So you have. Next Christmas will be deadly dull without such a special wish as this year," Anthony said with a laugh and a loving glance at Sarah.

"Oh, Alistair and I have another wish for next Christmas," Melissa announced in spite of her brother's glare.

"Another wish? What would that be?" Anthony asked, pausing at the door of the room.

"Melissa!" Alistair protested.

Ignoring her brother, Melissa said, "Next Christmas, we would like a new baby. A sister. Alistair said—"

"Melissa!" he protested again in a strangled voice.

Anthony tried to control the laughter that bubbled up inside him as he stared at Sarah, her cheeks red again. "I shall discuss Alistair's explanation with him later, Melissa."

"But can we have a new baby?"

"We will certainly do our best," he assured his daughter even as he pulled his new wife to him and kissed her deeply. "After all, the Christmas Angel granted our wish this Christmas. You have the most beautiful mama in the world."

Sarah wrapped one arm around his waist and the other around the two children staring up at her. "It is never too soon to begin wishing for wonderful things, Melissa. But we must not be too greedy. The Christmas Angel has already given us so much."

"I don't think a baby is too much to ask for," Melissa argued. "Angels like babies. After all, Jesus was a baby."

"How true. Very well, we shall ask for a baby," Anthony concurred. "And I promise to do my very best to help that wish come true." He stared at Sarah, his eyes filled with love, and she reached up to kiss him once more.

"May your wish come true," she murmured before urging them all through the door. "Come, let's bid everyone Happy Christmas. It is a very special time of year."

And shouts of joy rang through the halls of Whitfield House on Christmas morning.

**Fifty red-blooded, white-hot, true-blue hunks
from every State in the Union!**

Look for MEN MADE IN AMERICA! Written by some of our most poplar authors, these stories feature fifty of the strongest, sexiest men, each from a different state in the union!

Two titles available every other month at your favorite retail outlet.

In January, look for:

DREAM COME TRUE by Ann Major (Florida)
WAY OF THE WILLOW by Linda Shaw (Georgia)

In March, look for:

TANGLED LIES by Anne Stuart (Hawaii)
ROGUE'S VALLEY by Kathleen Creighton (Idaho)

You won't be able to resist MEN MADE IN AMERICA!

Relive the romance...
Harlequin and Silhouette
are proud to present

by Request™

A program of collections of three complete novels by the most requested
authors with the most requested themes. Be sure to look for one volume each
month with three complete novels by top name authors.

In January: **WESTERN LOVING**   Susan Fox
                                        JoAnn Ross
                                        Barbara Kaye

Loving a cowboy is easy—taming him isn't!

In February: **LOVER, COME BACK!**   Diana Palmer
                                        Lisa Jackson
                                        Patricia Gardner Evans

It was over so long ago—yet now they're calling, "Lover, Come Back!"

In March: **TEMPERATURE RISING**   JoAnn Ross
                                        Tess Gerritsen
                                        Jacqueline Diamond

Falling in love—just what the doctor ordered!

Available at your favorite retail outlet.

REQ-G3

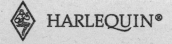 HARLEQUIN®   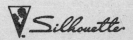 Silhouette

My Valentine 1994

Celebrate the most romantic day of the year with
MY VALENTINE 1994
a collection of original stories, written by
four of Harlequin's most popular authors...

MARGOT DALTON
MURIEL JENSEN
MARISA CARROLL
KAREN YOUNG

*Available in February, wherever
Harlequin Books are sold.*

 HARLEQUIN ®

VAL94

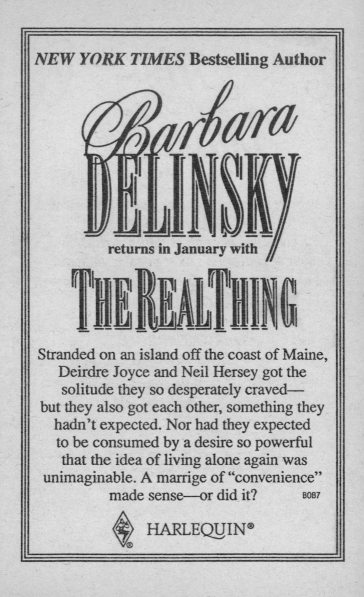

NEW YORK TIMES **Bestselling Author**

Barbara DELINSKY

returns in January with

THE REAL THING

Stranded on an island off the coast of Maine,
Deirdre Joyce and Neil Hersey got the
solitude they so desperately craved—
but they also got each other, something they
hadn't expected. Nor had they expected
to be consumed by a desire so powerful
that the idea of living alone again was
unimaginable. A marrige of "convenience"
made sense—or did it?

B0B7

HARLEQUIN®